GREAT HORSE STORIES

Great Horse Stories

Selected by
PAMELA MACGREGOR-MORRIS

Illustrated by
SUSAN PARES

HILL AND WANG - NEW YORK

Library of Congress catalog card number 61–16869

Printed in the United States of America

Contents

Smoky's Homecoming   11
Will James

Hard Times (from *Black Beauty*)   19
Anna Sewell

St Margaret of Ives (from *The Silver Horn*)   30
Gordon Grand

Mr. Pickwick as a Whip (from *The Pickwick Papers*)   37
Charles Dickens

Major Yeates buys The Quaker and Takes to Hunting   39
(from *Some Experiences of an Irish R.M.*)
E. O'E. Somerville and Martin Ross

An Irish Hunt (from *A Long Way to Go*)   56
Marigold Armitage

The Baron and His Horse (from *The Travels of Baron*   76
Münchausen
Anon

Somewhere in France (from *Broncho*)   78
Richard Ball

The Dealer's Yard (from *Mr Facey Romford's Hounds*)   94
R. S. Surtees

A Misdeal (from *Some Experiences of an Irish R.M.*)   97
E. O'E. Somerville and Martin Ross

Mr Soapey Goes Horse-Coping (from *Mr Sponge's*   102
Sporting Tour)
R. S. Surtees

'Your Handwriting, Sir' (from *Market Harborough*)   116
G. J. Whyte-Melville

Cahirmee Fair (from *Huic Holloa!*)   124
    'Spider' Jacobson

The White Knight on Equitation (from *Alice Through*   134
    the Looking Glass)
    Lewis Carroll

The First Ride (from *Lavengro*)   137
    George Borrow

Mr Pickwick as a Horseman (from *Pickwick Papers*)   141
    Charles Dickens

The Colonel's Cup (from *Memoirs of a Fox-Hunting Man*)   146
    Siegfried Sassoon

The Christening of Hildebrand (from *Hildebrand*)   154
    John Thorburn

Phari the Pony and Thunder the Mule (from *Phari—*   166
    The Adventures of a Tibetan Pony)
    M. E. Buckingham

Melka is Stolen by Gypsies (from *Melka in England*)   176
    Joan Penney

Modestine (from *Travels with a Donkey*)   189
    R. L. Stevenson

A Grown-up Could Hardly Have Stood It (from *The*   201
    Autobiography of Lincoln Steffens)

The Highwayman's Mare (from *Lorna Doone*)   207
    R. D. Blackmore

Three Hunting Songs *G. J. Whyte-Melville*   212
    The Clipper that Stands in the Stall at the Top
    The Good Grey Mare
    The Place Where the Old Horse Died

Mr Jorrocks Crosses a Country (from *Handley Cross*)   219
    R. S. Surtees

Acknowledgments

I should like to thank Longmans, Green & Co., Ltd., for permission to use the extracts from *Some Experiences of an Irish R.M.*, by E. O'E. Somerville and Martin Ross; Faber & Faber, Ltd., for excerpts from Siegfried Sassoon's *Memoirs of a Fox-Hunting Man* and Marigold Armitage's *A Long Way to Go;* Methuen, Ltd., for the extract from *Melka in England;* Mr. Richard Ball for part of *Broncho* and M. E. Buckingham for some of the story of *Phari, the Pony.*

"Smoky's Homecoming" is reprinted with the permission of Charles Scribner's Sons from *Smoky* by Will James. Copyright 1926 Charles Scribner's Sons; renewal copyright 1954 Auguste Dufault.

"A Grown-up Could Hardly Have Stood It," from *The Autobiography of Lincoln Steffens,* copyright 1931 by Harcourt, Brace & World, Inc.; renewed 1959 by Peter Steffens, is reprinted by permission of the publishers.

Introduction

This collection of horse and pony stories for children between the ages of twelve and sixteen has been selected both from the classical and modern fields.

Although the horse is man's oldest and possibly his best friend, very little really good literature is concerned with him. This seems especially true of present-day writing. A great many books about horses and ponies are published each year, but few of them go into more than one edition and fewer still will live on through the years as have the tales of authors of days gone by.

In compiling an anthology of horse and pony stories one is therefore faced with two alternatives. Either one explores a new field, in which the pickings are somewhat lean, or one sticks to the tried and trusted favourites.

I have tried to steer a middle course between the two schools, and I have also included some excerpts from some of the better children's pony books—a field that is virtually untapped. I hope that my readers will find something to interest them both in the tales of days gone by and in those of the present day.

Smoky's Homecoming

BY WILL JAMES

THE last day of the rodeo had come, and Clint was to start with his train-load of stock that night. Him and his friend was setting in the lobby of the hotel that evening a-talking and wondering when they'd be seeing one another again, when outside and by the telegraph pole came the same old mouse-coloured horse and stopped not an inch from where the two men had seen him a couple of days before.

Both was quick to spot him again this time, and right then, for some reason or other, the conversation died down. The first sight of that old pony hadn't been forgot, and when he showed up again this second time, right before their eyes, he was like reminding 'em, and natural-like set the two men to thinking. That old shadow of a horse told some of the hard knocks of life, of things that was past and gone and which could of been bettered while the bettering could be done.

It was while the thinking was going on that way, that Clint sort of felt a faint, faraway something a-knocking and from down the bottom of his think-tank. That something was trying hard to come back to life as that man's eyes kept a-going over the pony's blazed face and bony frame, but it was buried so far underneath so many things that'd been stacked there that the knocking was pretty well muffled up. It'd have to be helped by some sort of a sudden jolt before it could come out on top.

The jolt came as the vegetable man got his seat on the wagon and as usual reached for the whip. Clint's friend, a-trying to keep him from running out and starting a rumpus, had tried to draw his interest by asking:

'What's become of that cow-horse *Smoky*, that used to——?'

But the question was left for *him* to wonder about, for Clint wasn't there to answer. Instead the hotel door slammed and only a glimpse of that same cowboy could be seen as he passed by the lobby window. In less than it takes to tell it, he was up on the wagon, took a bulldogging holt of the surprised vegetable man, and by his whiskers drug him off his seat and down to earth.

The telephone on the desk of the sheriff's office rang until it near danced a jig, and when that feller lifted the receiver a female voice was heard to holler: 'Somebody is killing somebody else with a whip, by the Casa Grande Hotel. *Hurry! Quick!*'

The sheriff appeared on the scene and took in the goings on at a glance. Like a man who knowed his business, his eyes went to looking for what might of caused the argument as he came. He looked at the old horse whose frame showed through the hide, then the whip-marks on that hide. He knowed horses as well as he did men; and when he noticed more marks of the same whip on the bewhiskered man's face he stood his ground, watched, and then grinned.

'Say, cowboy,' he finally says, 'don't scatter that hombre's remains too much. You know we got to keep record of that kind same as if it was a white man, and I don't want to be looking all over the streets to find out who he *was*.'

Clint turned at the sound of the voice, and sizing up the grinning sheriff, went back to his victim and broke the butt-end of the whip over his head; after which he wiped his hands and proceeded to unhook the old horse off the wagon.

That evening was spent in 'investigating'. Clint and the sheriff went to the chicken-house man and found out enough from him about the vegetable man and his way of treating horses to put that hombre in a cool place and keep him there for a spell.

'I'm glad to've caught on to that feller's doings,' remarks the sheriff as him and Clint went to the livery stable, their next place of investigation.

There Clint listened mighty close as he learned a heap about the mouse-coloured horse when he was known as Cloudy. The stableman went on to tell as far as he knowed about the horse and the whole history of him, and when that pony was known thru the south-west and many other places as *The Cougar*, the wickedest bucking horse and fighting outlaw the country had ever layed eyes on.

Clint was kinda proud in hearing that. He's heard of The Cougar and that pony's bucking ability even up to the Canadian line and acrost it, and to himself he says: 'That Smoky horse never did do things half-ways.' But he got to wondering, and then asked how come the pony had turned out to be that kind of horse. That, the stable man didn't know. It was news to him that the horse had ever been anything else, and as he says:

'The first that was seen of that horse is when some cow-boys found him on the desert, amongst a bunch of wild horses, and packing a saddle. Nobody had ever showed up to claim him, and as that pony had been more than inclined to buck and fight is how come he was sold as a bucking horse—and, believe me, old-timer,' went on the stableman, shaking his head, 'he was *some* bucking horse.'

'Well,' sayd the sheriff, 'that's another clue run to the ground with nothing left of, but the remains.'

That night, the big engine was hooked on to the train-load of cattle as to per schedule and started puffing its way on to the north. In the last car, the one next to the caboose and the least crowded, a space had been partitioned off. In that space was a bale of good hay, a barrel of water, and an old mouse-coloured horse.

The winter that came was very different to any the old mouse-coloured horse had ever put in. The first part of it went by with him like in a trance, not realizing and hardly seeing. His old heart had dwindled down till only a sputtering flame was left, and that threatened to go out with the first hint of any kind of a breeze.

Clint had got the old horse in a warm box-stall, filled the manger full of the best blue joint hay there was, and even bedded him down with more of the same; water was in that same stall and where it could be easy reached, and then that cowboy had bought many a dollar's worth of condition powders, and other preparations which would near coax life back even in a dead body.

Two months went by when all seemed kinda hopeless, but Clint worked on and kept a-hoping. He'd brought the old horse in the house and made him a bed by the stove if that would of helped; and far as that goes, he'd of done anything else, just so a spark of life showed in the old pony's eyes; but he'd done all he could do, and as he'd lay a hand on the old skinny-neck and felt of the old hide, he'd cuss and wish for the chance of twisting out of shape who all had been responsible. Then his expression would change, and he'd near burst out crying as he'd think back and compare the old wreck with what that horse had been.

As much as Clint had liked Smoky, the old wreck of a shadow of that horse wasn't wanting for any of the same liking. It was still in the cowboy's heart a-plenty, and if anything more so, on account that the old pony was now needing help and a friend like he'd never needed before; and Clint was more on hand with the horse, now that he was worthless, than he'd been when Smoky was the four-hundred-dollar cow-horse and worth more.

Finally, and after many a day of care and worrying, Clint began to notice with a glad smile that the pony's hide was loosening up. Then after a week or so more of shoving hay and grain, condition powders and other things down the old pony's throat, a layer of meat begin to spread over them bones and under that hide. Then one day a spark showed in the pony's eyes, soon after that he started taking interest in the things around.

As layer after layer of meat and then tallow accumulated and rounded the sharp corners of Smoky's frame, that pony was for noticing more and more till after a while his interest spread enough, and with a clearer vision, went as far as to take in the man who kept a-going and coming, once in a while touched him, and then talked.

Clint liked to had a fit one day, when talking to the horse and happened to say *Smoky*, he noticed that pony cock an ear.

The recuperating of the horse went pretty fast from then on; and as the winter days howed past and early spring drawed near, there was no more fear of Smoky's last stand being anywheres near. As the days growed longer and the sun got warmer, there was times when Clint would lead the horse out and turn him loose to walk around in the sunshine, and that way get the blood to circulating. Smoky would sometimes mosey along for hours around the place and then start out on some trail, but always when the sun went

down he was by the stable door again and then Clint would
let him in.

Clint would watch him by the hour whenever the horse
was out that way, and he'd wonder, as he kept his eye on
him, if that pony remembered, if the knocks he'd got from
different countries didn't forever make him forget his home
range and all that went with it. Not many miles away was
where he was born; the big mountains now covered with
snow was the same he was raised on, and which he tore up
with his hoofs as he played while a little colt, and by his
mammy. The corrals by the stable and sheds was the ones
he was first run into when branded, and in them, a few
years later, broke to saddle; but what Clint would wonder
the most, as he watched, is whether Smoky remembered
him.

The cowboy had kept a-hoping that sometime he'd be
greeted with a nicker as he'd open the stable door in the
morning. Clint felt if the horse remembered, he would
nicker that way at the sight of him and like he used to; but
morning after morning went by, and even though Smoky
seemed full of life and rounded out to near natural again, no
nicker was ever heard.

'Somebody must of stretched that pony's heartstrings to
the breaking point,' he remarked one day, as he'd stopped,
wondering as usual, and looked at the horse.

Finally spring came sure enough, and broke up the winter.
Green grass-covered ridges took the place of snow-banks,
and the cottonwoods along the creeks was beginning to bud.
It was during one of them fine spring days, when riding
along and looking the country over, Clint run acrost a
bunch of horses. In the bunch was a couple of colts just a few
days old, and knowing that old ponies have such a strong
interest and liking for the little fellers, the cowboy figgered
the sight of them would help considerable in bringing
Smoky's heart up a few notches, and maybe to remembering.
He fell in behind the bunch and hazed 'em all towards the

corrals, and as Smoky, turned loose that day, spotted the bunch, his head went up. Then he noticed the little fellers and that old pony, gathering all the speed there was in him, headed straight for the bunch and amongst 'em.

Clint corralled him and all the rest together and setting on his horse at the gate, watched Smoky while that horse was having the time of his life getting acquainted. The pony dodged kicks and bites and went back and forth thru the bunch, and a spark showed in his eye which hadn't been there for many a day.

The cowboy could near see the horse smile at the little colts; and he was surprised at the show of action and interest the old pony had reserved, or gained. He was acting near like a two-year-old, and Clint grinned as he watched.

'Daggone his old hide,' says the cowboy. 'It looks to me like he'd good to live and enjoy life for many summers yet'; then thinking strong, he went on, 'And maybe in that time he might get to remembering me again—I wonder.'

He watched Smoky a while longer and till he got· acquainted some, and at last deciding it'd be best to let him go he reined his horse out of the gate and let the bunch run by. The old pony seemed to hesitate some as the bunch filed out. He liked their company mighty well but something held him back; then a horse nickered, and even though that nicker might not of been meant for him, it was enough to make him decide. He struck out on a high lope and towards the bunch, one of the little colts and full of play waited for him, and nipping the old horse in the flanks, run by his side till the bunch was caught up with—Smoky was *living* again.

Clint sat on his horse and watched the bunch lope out over a ridge and out of sight; and with a last glimpse at the mouse-coloured rump he grinned a little, but it was a sorry grin, and as he kept looking the way Smoky had gone, he says:

'I wonder if he ever will.'

.   .   .   .   .

With the green grass growing near an inch a day, Clint wasn't worried much on how old Smoky was making it. He figgered a horse couldn't die if he wanted to, not on that range at that time of the year; but some day soon he was going to try and locate the old horse and find out for sure how he really was. Then a lot of work came on which kept the cowboy from going out soon as he wanted to, and then one morning bright and early, as he stepped out to get a bucket of water, the morning sun throwed a shadow on the door; and as he stuck his head out a nicker was heard.

Clint dropped his bucket in surprise at what he heard and then seen. For, standing out a-ways, slick and shiny, was the mouse-coloured horse. The good care the cowboy had handed him, and afterwards the rambling over the old home range, had done its work. The heart of Smoky had come to life again, and full size.

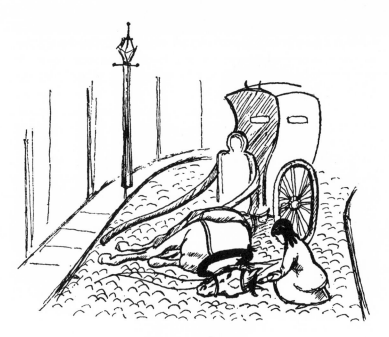

Hard Times

BY ANNA SEWELL

I SHALL never forget my new master. He had black eyes and a hooked nose; his mouth was as full of teeth as a bulldog's, and his voice was as harsh as the grinding of cart-wheels over gravel-stones. His name was Nicholas Skinner, and I believe he was the same man for whom poor Seedy Sam had driven.

I have heard men say that seeing is believing; but I should say that *feeling* is believing; for much as I had seen before, I never knew till now the utter misery of a cab-horse's life.

Skinner had a low set of cabs and a low set of drivers; he was hard on the men, and the men were hard on the horses. In this place we had no Sunday rest, and it was in the heat of summer.

Sometimes on a Sunday morning a party of fast men

would hire a cab for the day—four of them inside and another with the driver, and I had to take them ten or fifteen miles out into the country, and back again: never would any of them get down to walk up a hill, let it be ever so steep or the day ever so hot—unless, indeed, when the driver was afraid I should not manage it, and sometimes I was so fevered and worn that I could hardly touch my food. How I used to long for the nice bran mash with nitre in it that Jerry used to give us on Saturday nights in hot weather, that used to cool us down and make us so comfortable. Then we had two nights and a whole day for unbroken rest, and on Monday morning we were as fresh as young horses again; but here, there was no rest, and my driver was just as hard as his master.

He had a cruel whip with something so sharp at the end that it sometimes drew blood, and he would even whip me under the belly, and flip out the lash at my head. Indignities like these took the heart out of me terribly, but still I did my best and never hung back; for, as poor Ginger said, it was no use; men are the stronger.

My life was now so utterly wretched that I wished I might, like Ginger, drop down dead at my work, and so be out of misery; and one day my wish very nearly came to pass.

I went on the stand at eight in the morning, and had done a good share of work when we had to take a fare to the railway. A long train was just expected in, so my driver pulled up at the back of some of the outside cabs to take the chance of a return fare. It was a very heavy train, and as all the cabs were soon engaged, ours was called for.

There was a party of four: a noisy, blustering man with a lady, a little boy, a young girl and a great deal of luggage. The lady and the little boy got into the cab, and while the man ordered about the luggage, the young girl came and looked at me.

'Papa,' she said, 'I am sure this poor horse cannot take us

and all our luggage so far; he is so very weak and worn out; do look at him.'

'Oh! he's all right, miss,' said my driver, 'he's strong enough.'

The porter, who was pulling about some heavy boxes, suggested to the gentleman that, as there was so much luggage, he should take a second cab.

'Can your horse do it, or can't he?' said the blustering man.

'Oh! he can do it all right, sir. Send up the boxes, porter; he can take more than that.' Saying this, he helped to haul up a box so heavy that I could feel the springs go down.

'Papa, papa, do take a second cab,' said the young girl in a beseeching tone; 'I am sure we are wrong; I am sure it is very cruel.'

'Nonsense, Grace get in at once, and don't make all this fuss; a pretty thing it would be if a man of business had to examine every cab-horse before he hired it—the man knows his own business of course; there, get in and hold your tongue!'

My gentle friend had to obey; and box after box was dragged up and lodged on the top of the cab, or settled by the side of the driver. At last all was ready, and with his usual jerk of the rein and slash of the whip, he drove out of the station.

The load was very heavy, and I had had neither food nor rest since the morning; but I did my best, as I always had done in spite of cruelty and injustice.

I got along fairly until we came to Ludgate Hill; but there, the heavy load and my own exhaustion were too much. I was struggling to keep on, goaded by constant chucks of the rein and use of the whip, when, in a single moment—I cannot tell how—my feet slipped from under me and I fell heavily to the ground on my side. The suddenness and the force with which I fell seemed to beat all the breath out of my body.

I lay perfectly still; indeed, I had no power to move, and I thought now I was going to die. I heard a sort of confusion round me—loud, angry voices, and the getting down of the luggage, but it was all like a dream. I thought I heard that sweet, pitiful voice saying, 'Oh! that poor horse! It is all our fault.'

Someone came and loosened the throat strap of my bridle, and undid the traces which kept the collar so tight upon me. Someone said, 'He's dead, he'll never get up again.' Then I could hear a policeman giving orders, but I did not even open my eyes; I could only draw a gasping breath now and then. Some cold water was thrown over my head, some cordial was poured into my mouth, and something was covered over me.

I cannot tell how long I lay there, but I found my life coming back, and a kind-voiced man was patting me and encouraging me to rise. After some more cordial had been given me, and after one or two attempts, I staggered to my feet, and was gently led to some stables which were close by. Here I was put into a well-littered stall, and some warm gruel was brought to me: this I drank thankfully.

In the evening I was sufficiently recovered to be led back to Skinner's stables, where I think they did the best for me they could. In the morning Skinner came with a farrier (veterinary surgeon) to look at me. He examined me very closely, and said:

'This is a case of overwork more than disease, and if you could give him a run-off for six months, he would be able to work again; but now there is not an ounce of strength in him.'

'Then he must just go to the dogs,' said Skinner. 'I have no meadows to nurse sick horses in—he may get well or he may not; that sort of thing does not suit my business. My plan is to work 'em as long as they'll go, and then sell 'em for what they'll fetch at the knacker's or elsewhere.'

'If he was broken-winded,' said the farrier, 'you had better have had him killed out of hand, but he is not; there is a sale of horses coming off in about ten days; if you rest him and feed him up, he may pick up, and you may at any rate get more than his skin is worth.'

Upon this advice Skinner, rather unwillingly, I think, gave orders that I should be well fed and cared for; and the stableman, happily for me, carried out the orders with a much better will than his master had shown in giving them.

Ten days of perfect rest, plenty of good oats, hay and bran mashes with boiled linseed mixed in them, did more to get up my condition than anything else could have done. Those linseed mashes were delicious, and I began to think that after all it might be better to live than go to the dogs. When the twelfth day after the accident came, I was taken to the sale, a few miles out of London. I felt that any change from my present place must be an improvement; so I held up my head, and hoped for the best.

At this sale, of course, I found myself in company with the old broken-down horses—some lame, some broken-winded, some old, and some that I am sure it would have been merciful to shoot.

The buyers and sellers, too, many of them, looked not much better off than the poor beasts for which they were bargaining. There were poor old men trying to get a horse or pony for a few pounds to drag about some little wood or coal cart. There were poor men trying to sell a worn-out beast for two or three pounds, rather than have the greater loss of killing him.

Some of them looked as if poverty and hard times had hardened them all over; but there were others for whom I would willingly have used the last of my strength—poor and shabby, but kind and human, with voices that I could trust. There was one tottering old man that took a great fancy to me, and I to him, but I was not strong enough—it was an anxious time!

Coming from the better part of the fair, I noticed a man

who looked like a gentleman farmer, with a young boy by his side. He had a broad back and round shoulders, a kind, ruddy face, and he wore a broad-brimmed hat. When he came up to me and my companions, he stood still and gave a pitiful look round upon us. I saw his eye rest on me; I had still a good mane and tail, which did something for my appearance. I pricked my ears and looked at him.

'There's a horse, Willie, that has known better days.'

'Poor old fellow!' said the boy. 'Do you think, grandpa, he was ever a carriage horse?'

'Oh, yes, my boy,' said the farmer, coming closer, 'he might have been anything when he was young. Look at his nostrils and his ears, and the shape of his neck and shoulders; there's a good deal of breeding about that horse.' He put out his hand and gave me a kind pat on the neck. I put out my nose in answer to his kindness, and the boy stroked my face.

'Poor old fellow! See, grandpa, how well he understands kindness. Could you not buy him and make him young again, as you did Ladybird?'

'My dear boy, I can't make all old horses young. Besides, Ladybird was not so old as she was run down and badly used.'

'Well, grandpa, I don't believe that this one is old; look at his mane and tail. I wish you would look into his mouth, and then you could tell. Though he is so very thin, his eyes are not sunken like some old horses.'

The old gentleman laughed. 'Bless the boy! He is as horsy as his old grandfather!'

'But do look at his mouth, grandpapa, and ask the price; I am sure he would grow young in our meadows.'

The man who had brought me for sale now put in his word.

'The young gentleman's a real knowing one, sir. Now the fact is, this 'ere hoss is just pulled down with overwork in the cabs. He's not an old one, and I heard as how the vet should say that a six-months' runoff would set him right up, being as how his wind was not broken. I've had the tending of him these ten days past, and a more grateful and pleasant animal I have never met. 'Twould be worth a gentleman's while to give a five-pound note for him and let him have a chance. I'll be bound he'd be worth twenty pounds next spring.'

The old gentleman laughed, and the little boy looked up eagerly.

'Oh, grandpa, did you not say that the colt sold for five pounds more than you expected? You would not be poorer if you did buy this one.'

The farmer slowly felt my legs, which were much swollen and strained; then he looked at my mouth—'Thirteen or fourteen, I should say. Just trot him out, will you?'

I arched my poor thin neck, raised my tail a little, and threw my legs out as well as I could, for they were very stiff.

'What is the lowest you will take for him?' said the farmer as I came back.

'Five pounds, sir; that was the lowest price my master set.'

''Tis a speculation,' said the old gentleman, shaking his head, but at the same time slowly drawing out his purse. 'Quite a speculation! Have you any more business here?' he said, counting the sovereigns into the man's hand.

'No, sir, I can take him for you to the inn if you please.'

'Do so; I am now going there.'

They walked forward, and I was led behind. The boy could hardly control his delight, and the old gentleman seemed to enjoy his pleasure. I had a good feed at the inn, and was then gently ridden home by a servant of my new master and turned into a large meadow with a shed in one corner of it.

Mr Thoroughgood, for that was the name of my benefactor, gave orders that I should have hay and oats every night and morning, and the run of the meadow during the day. 'You, Willie,' said he, 'must take the oversight of him; I give him into your charge.'

The boy was proud of his charge, and undertook it in all seriousness. There was not a day when he did not pay me a visit, picking me out from among the other horses to give me a bit of carrot or some other good thing, or sometimes to stand by me whilst I ate my oats. He always came with kind words and caresses, and of course I grew very fond of him. He called me Old Crony, as I used to come to him in the field and follow him about. Sometimes he brought his grandfather, who always looked closely at my legs.

'That is our point, Willie,' he would say; 'but he is improving so steadily that I think we shall see a change for the better in the spring.'

The perfect rest, the good food, the soft turf, and gentle exercise soon began to tell on my condition and my spirits. I had a good constitution from my mother, and I was never strained when I was young, so that I had a better chance than many horses who have been worked before they came to their full strength.

During the winter my legs improved so much that I began to feel quite young again. The spring came round, and one day in March Mr Thoroughgood determined that he would try me in the phaeton. I was well pleased, and he and Willie drove me a few miles. My legs were not stiff now and I did the work with perfect ease.

'He's growing young, Willie; we must give him a little gentle work now, and by midsummer he will be as good as Ladybird; he has a beautiful mouth and good paces; these could not be better.'

'Oh, grandpapa, how glad I am you bought him!'

'So am I, my boy, but he has to thank you more than me. We must now be looking out for a quiet, genteel place for him where he will be valued.'

One day during this summer the groom cleaned and dressed me with such extraordinary care that I thought some new change must be at hand. He trimmed my fetlocks and legs, passed the tarbrush over my hoofs, and even parted my forelock. I think the harness also had an extra polish. Willie seemed half anxious, half merry, and he got into the chaise with his grandfather.

'If the ladies take to him,' said the old gentleman, 'they'll be suited, and he'll be suited: we can but try.'

At the distance of a mile or two from the village we came to a pretty, low house with a lawn and shrubbery at the front and a drive up to the door. Willie rang the bell, and asked if Miss Blomefield or Miss Ellen was at home. Yes, they both were. So whilst Willie stayed with me, Mr Thoroughood went into the house.

In about ten minutes he returned, followed by three ladies. One tall, pale lady, wrapped in a white shawl, leaned on a younger lady with dark eyes and a merry face; the third, a very stately-looking person, was Miss Blomefield. They all came to look at me and ask questions. The younger lady—this was Miss Ellen—took to me very much; she said she was sure she should like me, for I had such a good face. The tall, pale lady said that she should always be nervous in riding behind a horse that had once been down, as I might come down again; and if I did, she should never get over the fright.

'You see, ladies,' said Mr Thoroughgood, 'many first-rate horses have had their knees broken through the carelessness of their drivers, without any fault of their own; and from what I see of this horse, I should say that is his case: but, of course, I do not wish to influence you. If you wish, you can have him on trial, and then your coachman will see what he thinks of him.'

'You have always been such a good adviser to us about our horses,' said the stately lady, 'that your recommendation would go a long way with me, and if my sister Lavinia sees no objection, we will accept with thanks your offer of a trial.'

It was then arranged that I should be sent for the next day.

In the morning a smart-looking young man came for me. At first he looked pleased, but when he saw my knees he said in a disappointed voice: 'I didn't think, sir, you would have recommended my ladies a blemished horse like this.'

'Handsome is that handsome does,' said my master. 'You are only taking him on trial, and I am sure you will do fairly by him, young man; and if he is not as safe as any horse you ever drove, send him back.'

I was led home, placed in a comfortable stable, fed, and left to myself. The next day, when my groom was cleaning my face, he said? 'That is just like the star that Black Beauty had, and he is much the same height, too; I wonder where he is now?'

A little farther on he came to the place in my neck where I was bled, and where a little knot was left in the skin. He almost started, and began to look me over carefully, talking to himself.

'White star in the forehead, one white foot on the offside, this little knot just in that place'; then, looking at the middle of my back—'and as I am alive, there is that little patch of white hair that John used to call "Beauty's three-penny bit". It *must* be Black Beauty! Why, Beauty! Beauty! do you know me, little Joe Green that almost killed you?' And he began patting and patting me as if he was quite overjoyed.

I could not say that I remembered him, for now he was a fine grown young fellow with black whiskers and a man's voice, but I was sure he knew me, and that he was Joe Green; so I was very glad. I put my nose up to him, and tried to say that we were friends. I never saw a man so pleased.

'Give him a fair trial! I should think so indeed! I wonder who the rascal was that broke your knees, my old Beauty! You must have been badly served out somewhere. Well, well, it won't be my fault if you haven't good times of it now. I wish John Manly were here to see you.'

In the afternoon I was put into a low park chair and

brought to the door. Miss Ellen was going to try me, and Green went with her. I soon found that she was a good driver, and she seemed pleased with my paces. I heard Joe telling her about me, and that he was sure I was Squire Gordon's old Black Beauty.

When we returned, the other sisters came out to hear how I had behaved myself. She told them what she had just heard, and said, 'I shall certainly write to Mrs Gordon and tell her that her favourite horse has come to us. How pleased she will be!'

After this I was driven every day for a week or so, and as I appeared to be quite safe, Miss Lavinia at last ventured out in the small close carriage. After this, it was decided to keep me and to call me by my old name of Black Beauty.

I have now lived in this happy place a whole year. Joe is the best and kindest of grooms. My work is easy and pleasant, and I feel my strength and spirits all coming back again. Mr Thoroughgood said to Joe the other day, 'In your place he will last till he is twenty years old—perhaps more.'

Willie always speaks to me when he can, and treats me as his special friend. My ladies have promised that I shall never be sold, and so I have nothing to fear; and here my story ends. My troubles are all over and I am at home; and often before I am quite awake, I fancy I am still in the orchard at Birtwick, standing with my old friends under the apple trees.

(From *Black Beauty*).

St Margaret of Ives

BY GORDON GRAND

HE arrived with his horse on Thursday. On Saturday the manager of the riding academy received word that the Polish officer had been taken ill. Three days later he answered his final roll-call.

I never saw him, but they said that the two nurses who attended him at the hospital knelt at the bedside when it was all over, and wept, and that the surgeon told an associate going down in the elevator that the young Polish officer was the most engaging personality he had ever encountered.

The hospital, not knowing what else to do, communicated with the Polish Consulate from whence a supercilious and indifferent young man arrived to give directions and take charge of the personal effects. From the hospital the bored young diplomat proceded to a scanty room in a meagre boarding house in Brooklyn. What it was he discovered there I never learned, but the young man came out of the lodging house at double-quick time, headed for the nearest telephone, called up his superior who, in turn, started the wires humming to Washington, and the cables humming to Poland, and within the hour two very elderly and dignified persons arrived to take charge. That's all I know of the matter.

A week later Tom Murdock took time from his law practice to write me as follows:

'Dear PENDLETON,

'There is the sweetest blood mare I have ever set my eyes on for sale at the Academy. I understand she belonged to some foreign officer who died, or something, so they must get rid of her. Five hundred dollars will do the trick. Why don't you run down and see her? She is just your kind.

'Hastily,
'TOM MURDOCK'.

I ran down, rode and jumped the mare, became more enamoured than I have ever been of any horse before or since, and bought her. As I entered my taxi after completing the transaction I remembered that I had failed to ascertain the mare's name, so I went back and asked the manager. He consulted his book and said, 'St Margaret of Ives'. She arrived at my farm on May 25th. On the 26th I started by motor to meet Colonel Weatherford at his Canadian salmon water.

I was clipping off the miles through the Province of Quebec when at about four o'clock in the afternoon I came to a sizeable town. There had been a shower a few minutes before, making the streets slippery, and in avoiding a small boy with a bundle of afternoon newspapers under one arm, the rear wheel of my car hit a culvert and something let go. The sympathetic garage man said it would take two days—perhaps three—to procure the necessary parts from Montreal.

As we talked a passer-by stopped to look at the damaged car. Turning, I recognized him at once. I would have known him among ten million. Twenty-six years ago he had attended a convention as a delegate from the McGill chapter of my faternity, and we had seen much of each other. He had come over from England to Canada, where his people had important holdings, and entered the Canadian university, planning to settle in the country after graduation.

Of course I recognized him, for I had been more impressed and influenced by him than by any fellow student I had ever met. He was a famous athlete—a fine sportsman, and above all, a born leader though of a quiet, retiring disposition. I gleaned some lessons from his book, and gleaned them so thoroughly that his precepts had become a very part of me, and there he was standing looking at my wrecked car.

I called him by name, stepped forward and held out my hand. He had no idea who I was, but his face lit up with the gay spontaneous smile I remembered so well. When I recalled our meeting years ago a tinge of pain came over his face—pain that he should have forgotten even a casual acquaintance—and he carried me off to his home to stay until my car could be repaired. It was a spacious, generous brick house set in a landscaped park, for he was the man of affairs in that district. He had lived up to the promise of his youth.

At tea-time we were joined by his wife, a courtly, yet cordial and gracious woman. At dinner I was presented to the daughter, Margaret, a tall fair-haired girl of twenty-two, just returned from a long stay abroad. She was a striking girl, and as father and daughter stood together with their backs to the fireplace waiting for dinner to be announced I thought them the handsomest pair I had seen in many years. After dinner my host and hostess were under the necessity of attending some local meeting, and the daughter and I were to entertain one another pending their return.

There was a twang in the air of that far north country

even in May so we pulled our chairs up to the open grate in which great chunks of cannel coal were burning. It is not always easy for youth and middle age to converse together throughout an evening, yet on this evening I lamented the too quick passage of time. She had much of her father's ardour and enthusiasm—his love of sport, fair play and tolerance but, above all, a deep Catholic sympathy for all who were oppressed.

During two intensive years she had been seeing Europe under auspices which only strong diplomatic connections can make possible. She returned confounded by the century-old hates of neighbouring peoples, and her sympathy aflame for those who lived under alien yokes—the Poles and all others whose heritage had been sold or bartered away.

We finally drifted into a discussion of military equitation as practised in the different armies and she had just finished a vivid and telling description of a memorable gathering of cavalry officers of many nations and the magnificent riding of each, when the thought struck me that I should get a telegram through to Colonel Weatherford. In the excitement of the afternoon I had never ascertained even the name of the town I was staying in, so I asked her. 'This is Ives,' she said.

She was sitting on a low bench with her back to the fire, but her head turned towards the fireplace. I don't know whether I spoke to her or was only reflecting aloud, but I said, half to myself, 'St Margaret of Ives'. I was not looking at her when I said this, yet sensed that she made a quick movement. When I looked up she was staring at me with wide-open eyes and quite plainly grasping the side of the bench with her hands. My remark seemed innocent enough to me, yet I could only conclude that she resented my seeming familiarity. I arose, went to a near-by table and thinking to make amends, said, 'You know, I have just acquired a little bay mare called St Margaret of Ives.'

As I mentioned, I was standing up and lighting my pipe

when I said this. The next thing I knew she was standing in front of me. 'You—you own her,' she said, and there was a tenseness in her voice nothing short of alarming. 'How could you have her? You couldn't. It can't be the same one. Quick! Tell me about her.' As she spoke she kept coming closer and closer to me, until she finally took hold of one of the buttons of my coat and twisted it nervously, while her great, inquiring eyes searched deeply into me. I told her the little that I knew.'

She was of magnificent courage. There was no display of what was going on within her. She asked me if I minded being alone, said 'good-night', turned and walked towards the door. Then she stopped, stood a moment, came back to me, took the lapels of my coat in her hands and said, 'Are you fond of her?'

'Yes,' I said, 'very fond.'

'Do you intend to keep her always?'

'Always,' I answered.

'Thank you,' she said, and left me. I never saw her again. Within the year the Convent of St Cecilia received a noviatiate.

The fall of that year came. I am grateful for the gift of memory which keeps for-ever green the myriad of happy characteristics of horses and dogs who meant much to me and grew old in my companionship. Of all my cherished memories of sport there is none more companionable than the autumn-tinted picture of the one and only one hunting season little St Margaret of Ives and I ever had together. My mind never reverts to fox-hunting of long ago but I see the little mare with her bewitchingly beautiful head and ingratiating ways. I contemplate even now the way she had of playing with her bit as she stepped so airily and lightly along; her intense way of turning her head whenever a hound opened and concentrating her entire being upon the sound; then when naught would come of it, turning her head away with what always sounded to me like a monstrous sigh; her teasing to go always a trifle faster, yet never taking hold of her bit; her willingness to creep to her fences when creeping was necessary and her boldness in standing away and flying them when the going was good. I was forever amused at her pressing desire to get to hounds by the most direct route, and her intolerance of my more conventional way. I am told that there are people whose ears are deaf to the music of horses' feet in new-fallen oak leaves—big, crisp, crinkly leaves—people unable to distinguish the gay rustling of thoroughbred feet from the dull listless thud of big-footed half-bred Irishmen. Why, St Margaret's feet played a veritable autumn symphony through the leaves.

Thanksgiving Day finally arrived, a day that marked the high point of achievement of all time for our hounds and foxes. The day's events have become a legend. At four-thirty in the afternoon, when not above three-quarters of an hour of daylight was left, only six from a field of seventy remained with hounds. At a quarter to five only Enid Ashley, Colonel Weatherford and I laboured up the western slope of Pugsley Hill. At the summit Enid's Jack Knife and the Colonel's Matchmaker stopped and I went down the western slope alone with hounds.

It is all very well for people to say that I never should have done it but they who criticize never felt that bay mare under them. She was a law unto herself. She started down that long, far-reaching hill with such buoyancy and supreme courage that I thought we were invulnerable. She instilled me with such exhilaration that day I became as another person. Then, it let go. I jumped off. I knew what it was. No tendon on earth could support indefinitely so high and valiant a courage.

I stood beside her with my hand resting on her wither and together we watched hounds race on towards the setting sun. Down through all the years I can see those small, sensitive, alert ears and great dark eyes following the fading hounds. When the final gleam of colour sank below the peak of

Stillings Mountain the sun had set for the last time for St Margaret of Ives afield. I led her away.

Last Thursday a car came to a sudden stop in front of my driveway. I saw the occupant of the car studying my name on the letter-box, then he looked towards the house and turned the car into the driveway. There he was, tall, erect, and now very grey. Motoring back from New York to Canada he was taking a detour through the Berkshires and had seen my name on the mail-box.

We sat together on the terrace through the hours of that so exquisite May afternoon talking of this and that, but I knew only too well that I conjured up an ancient wound that time could only partially heal.

As we talked, an old mare came round the corner of the house and went to cropping the rich grass under the apple trees. At each breath of air blossoms drifted down and nestled a while in the old matron's mane. 'Is she meant to be loose about the lawn like that?' he asked.

'Yes,' I said.

'Ah, an old favourite, I suppose?'

'Yes,' I replied. 'She is twenty-seven years old. I crippled her on a Thanksgiving Day twenty-one years ago.'

'What do you call her?' he asked. I hesitated, then pretended that I had not heard him, and we talked of other things.

(From *The Silver Horn*).

Mr Pickwick as a Whip

BY CHARLES DICKENS

'How old is that horse, my friend?' inquired Mr Pickwick, rubbing his nose with the shilling he had reserved for the fare.

'Forty-two,' replied the driver, eyeing him askant.

'What?' ejaculated Mr Pickwick, laying his head upon his notebook. . . . 'And how long do you keep him out at a time?'

'Two or three weeks,' replied the man.

'Weeks!' said Mr Pickwick in astonishment—and out came that notebook again.

'He lives at Pentonwil when he's at home,' observed the driver coolly, 'but we seldom takes him home on account of his weakness.'

'On account of his weakness?' reiterated the perplexed Mr Pickwick.

'He always falls down when he's took out o' the cab,' continued the driver, 'but when he's in it, we bears him up werry tight, and takes him in werry short, so as he can't werry well fall down; and we've got a pair o' precious large wheels on, so ven he *does* move, they run after him, and he must go on—he can't help it.'

Mr Pickwick entered every word of this statement in his notebook, with the view of communicating it to the Club, as a singular instance of the tenacity of the life of horses, under trying circumstances.

(From *The Pickwick Papers*).

Major Yeates buys The Quaker
and Takes to Hunting

BY E. O'E. SOMERVILLE AND MARTIN ROSS

ONLY those who have been through a similar experience
can know what manner of afternoon I spent. I am a martyr
to colds in the head, and I felt one coming on. I made a
laager in front of the dining-room fire, with a tattered
leather screen and the dinner-table, and gradually, with
cigarettes and strong tea, baffled the smell of must and cats,
and fervently trusted that the rain might avert a threatened
visit from my landlord. I was then but superficially acquainted with Mr Florence McCarthy Knox and his habits.

At about four-thirty when the room had warmed up and
my cold was yielding to treatment, Mrs Cadogan entered
and informed me that 'Mr Flurry' was in the yard, and

would be thankful if I'd go out to him, for he couldn't come in. Many are the privileges of the female sex; had I been a woman I should unhesitatingly have said that I had a cold in my head. Being a man, I huddled on a mackintosh and went out into the yard.

My landlord was there on horseback, and with him there was a man standing at the head of a stout grey animal. I recognized with despair that I was about to be compelled to buy a horse.

'Good afternoon, Major,' said Mr Knox in his slow, sing-song brogue; 'it's rather soon to be paying you a visit, but I thought you might be in a hurry to see the horse I was telling you of.'

I could have laughed. As if I were ever in a hurry to see a horse! I thanked him, and suggested that it was rather wet for horse-dealing.

'Oh, it's nothing when you're used to it,' replied Mr Knox. His gloveless hands were red and wet, the rain ran down his nose, and his covert coat was soaked to a sodden brown. I thought that I did not want to become used to it. My relations with horses have been of a purely military character. I have endured the Sandhurst riding-school, I have galloped for an impetuous general, I have been steward at regimental races, but none of these feats have altered my opinion that the horse, as a means of locomotion, is obsolete. Nevertheless, the man who accepts a resident magistracy in the south-west of Ireland voluntarily retires into the prehistoric age; to institute a stable becomes inevitable.

'You ought to throw a leg over him,' said Mr Knox, 'and you're welcome to take him over a fence or two if you like. He's a nice flippant jumper.'

Even to my unexacting eye the grey horse did not seem to promise flippancy, nor did I at all desire to find that quality in him. I explained that I wanted something to drive and not to ride.

'Well, that's a fine raking horse in harness,' said Mr

Knox, looking at me with his serious grey eyes, 'and you'd drive him with a sop of hay in his mouth. Bring him up here, Michael.'

Michael abandoned his efforts to kick the grey horse's forelegs into a becoming position, and led him up to me.

I regarded him from under my umbrella with a quite unreasonable disfavour. He had the dreadful beauty of a horse in a toyshop, as chubby, as wooden, and as conscientiously dappled, but it was unreasonable to urge this as an objection, and I was incapable of finding any more technical drawback. Yielding to circumstance, I 'threw my leg' over the brute, and after pacing gravely around the quadrangle that formed the yard, and jolting to my entrance gate and back, I decided that as he had neither fallen down nor kicked me off, it was worth paying twenty-five pounds for him, if only to get in out of the rain.

Mr Knox accompanied me into the house and had a drink. He was a fair, spare young man, who looked like a stable-boy among gentlemen, and a gentlemen among stable-boys. He belonged to a clan that cropped up in every grade of society in the country, from Sir Valentine Knox of Castle Knox down to the auctioneer Knox, who bore the attractive title of Larry the Liar. So far as I could judge, Florence McCarthy of that ilk occupied a shifting position about midway in the tribe. I had met him at dinner at Sir Valentine's, I had heard of him at an illicit auction, held by Larry the Liar, of brandy stolen from a wreck. They were 'Black Protestants', all of them, in virtue of their descent from a godly soldier of Cromwell, and all were prepared at any moment of the day or night to sell a horse.

ii

It is hardly creditable that I should have been induced to depart from my usual walk of life by a creature so uninspiring as the grey horse that I bought from Flurry Knox for twenty-five pounds.

Perhaps it was the monotony of being questioned by every other person with whom I had five minutes' conversation, as to when I was coming out with the hounds, and being further informed that in the days when Captain Browne, the late coastguard officer, had owned the grey, there was not a fence between this and Mallow big enough to please them. At all events, there came an epoch-making day when I mounted the Quaker and presented myself at a meet of Mr Knox's hounds. It is my belief that six out of every dozen people who go out hunting are disagreeably conscious of a nervous system, and two out of the six are in what is brutally called 'a blue funk'. I was not in a blue funk, but I was conscious not only of a nervous system, but of the anatomical fact that I possessed large, round legs, handsome in their way, even admirable in their proper sphere, but singularly ill-adapted for adhering to the slippery surfaces of a saddle. By a fatal intervention of Providence, the sport, on this my first day in the hunting-field, was such as I could have enjoyed from a bath-chair. The hunting-field was, on this occasion, a relative term, implying long stretches of unfenced moorland and bog—anything, in fact, save a field; the hunt itself might also have been termed a relative one, being mainly composed of Mr Knox's relations in all degrees of cousinhood. It was a day when frost and sunshine combined went to one's head like iced champagne: the distant sea looked like the Mediterranean, and for four sunny hours the Knox relatives and I followed nine couple of hounds at a tranquil footpace along the hills, our progress mildly enlivened by one or two scrambles in the shape of jumps. At three o'clock I jogged home, and felt within me the inborn desire to brag to Peter Cadogan of the Quaker's doings, as I dismounted rather stiffly in my own yard.

I little thought that the result would be that three weeks later I should find myself in a railway carriage at an early hour of a December morning, in company with Flurry Knox and four or five of his clan, journeying towards an unknown town, called Drumcurran, with an appropriate number of horses in boxes behind us and a van full of hounds in front. Mr Knox's hounds were on their way, by invitation, to have a day in the country of their neighbours, the Curranhilty Harriers, and with amazing fatuity I had allowed myself to be cajoled into joining the party. A northerly shower was striking in long spikes on the glass of the window, the atmosphere of the carriage was blue with tobacco smoke, and my feet, in a pair of new blucher boots, had sunk into a species of Arctic sleep.

'Well, you got my letter about the dance at the hotel tonight?' said Flurry Knox, breaking off a whispered conversation with his amateur whip, Dr Jerome Hickey, and sitting down beside me. 'And we're to go out with the Harriers today, and they've a sure fox for our hounds tomorrow. I tell you you'll have the best fun ever you had. It's a great country to ride. Fine honest banks, that you can come racing at anywhere you like.'

Dr Hickey, a saturine young man with a long nose and a black torpedo beard, returned to his pocket the lancet with which he had been trimming his nails.

'They're like the Tipperary banks,' he said; 'you climb down nine feet and you fall the rest.'

It occurred to me that the Quaker and I would probably fall all the way, but I said nothing.

'I hear Tomsy Flood has a good horse this season,' resumed Flurry.

'Then it's not the one you sold him,' said the doctor.

'I'll take my oath it's not,' said Flurry with a grin. 'I believe he has it in for me still over that one.'

Dr Jerome's moustache went up under his nose and showed his white teeth.

'Small blame to him! when you sold him a mare that was wrong of both her hind-legs. Do you know what he did,

Major Yeates? The mare was lame going into the fair, and
he took the two hind-shoes off her and told poor Flood she
kicked them off in the box, and that was why she was going
tender, and he was so drunk he believed him.'

The conversation here deepened into trackless obscurities
of horse-dealing. I took out my stylograph pen, and finished
a letter to Philippa, with a feeling that it would probably be
my last.

The next step in the day's enjoyment consisting in trotting
in cavalcade through the streets of Drumcurran, with
another northerly shower descending upon us, the mud
splashing in my face, and my feet coming torturingly to
life. Every man and boy in the town ran with us; the Harriers
were somewhere in the tumult ahead, and the Quaker began
to pull and hump his back ominously. I arrived at the meet
considerably heated, and found myself one of some thirty
or forty riders, who, with traps and bicycles and footpeople,
were jammed in a narrow, muddy road. We were late, and a
move was immediately made across a series of grass fields,
all considerately furnished with gates. There was a glacial
gleam of sunshine, and people began to turn down the
collars of their coats. As they spread over the field I observed
that Mr Knox was no longer riding with old Captain Hand-
cock, the Master of the Harriers, but had attached himself
to a square-shouldered young lady with effective coils of
dark hair and a grey habit. She was riding a fidgety black
mare with great decision and a not disagreeable swagger.

It was at about this moment that the hounds began to
run, fast and silently, and everyone began to canter.

'This is nothing at all,' said Dr Hickey, thundering along-
side of me on a huge young chestnut; 'there might have been
a hare here last week, or a red herring this morning. I
wouldn't care if we only got what'd warm us. For the matter
of that, I'd as soon hunt a cat as a hare.'

I was already getting quite enough to warm me. The
Quaker's respectable grey head had twice disappeared

between his forelegs in a brace of most unsettling bucks, and all my experiences in the riding-school at Sandhurst did not prepare me for the sensation of jumping a briary wall with a heavy drop into a lane so narrow that each horse had to turn at right angles as he landed. I did not so turn, but saved myself from entire disgrace by a timely clutch at the mane. We scrambled out of the lane over a pile of stones and furze bushes, and at the end of the next field were confronted by a tall, stone-faced bank. Everyone, always excepting myself, was riding with that furious valour which is so conspicuous when neighbouring hunts meet, and the leading half-dozen charged the obstacle at steeplechase speed. I caught a glimpse of the young lady in the grey habit, sitting square and strong as her mare topped the bank, with Flurry and the redoubtable Mr Tomsy Flood riding on either hand; I followed in their wake, with a blind confidence in the Quaker, and none at all in myself. He refused it. I suppose it was in token of affection and gratitude that I fell on his neck; at all events, I had reason to respect his judgement, as, before I had recovered myself, the hounds were struggling back into the field by a gap lower down.

It finally appeared that the hounds could do no more with the line they had been hunting, and we proceeded to jog interminably, I knew not whither. During this unpleasant process Flurry Knox bestowed on me many items of information, chiefly as to the pangs of jealousy he was inflicting on Mr Flood by his attentions to the lady in the grey habit, Miss 'Bobbie' Bennett.

'She'll have all old Hancock's money one of these days—she's his niece, y' know—and she's a good girl to ride, but she's not as young as she was ten years ago. You'd be looking at a chicken a long time before you thought of her! She might take Tomsy some day if she can't do any better.' He stopped and looked at me with a gleam in his eyes. 'Come on, and I'll introduce you to her!'

Before, however, this privilege could be mine, the whole

cavalcade was stopped by a series of distant yells, which apparently conveyed information to the hunt, though to me they only suggested a Red Indian scalping his enemy. The yells travelled rapidly nearer, and a young man with a scarlet face and a long stick sprang upon the fence, and explained that he and Patsy Lorry were after chasing a hare two miles down out of the hill above, and ne'er a dog nor a one with them but themselves, and she was lying, beat out, under a bush, and Patsy Lorry was minding her until the hounds would come. I had a vision of the humane Patsy Lorry fanning the hare with his hat, but apparently nobody else found this fact unusual. The hounds were hurried into the fields, the hare was again spurred into action, and I was again confronted with the responsibilities of the chase. After the first five minutes I had discovered several facts about the Quaker. If the bank was above a certain height he refused it irrevocably, if it accorded with his ideas he got his forelegs over and ploughed through the rest of it on his stifle-joints, or, if a gripe made this inexpedient, he remained poised on top till the fabric crumbled under his weight. In the case of walls he battered them down with his knees, or squandered them with his hind-legs. These operations took time, and the leaders of the hunt streamed farther and farther away over the crest of a hill, while the Quaker pursued at the equable gallop of a horse in the Bayeux Tapestry.

I began to perceive that I had been adopted as a pioneer by a small band of followers, who, as one of their number candidly explained, 'liked to have someone ahead of them to soften the banks', and accordingly waited respectfully till the Quaker had made the rough places smooth, and taken the raw edge off the walls. They, in their turn, showed me alternative routes when the obstacle proved above the Quaker's limit; thus, in ignoble confederacy, I and the off-scourings of the Curranhilty hunt pursued our way across some four miles of country. When at length we parted it was with extreme regret on both sides. A river crossed our course, with boggy banks pitted deep with the hoof-marks of our forerunners; I suggested it to the Quaker, and discovered that nature had not in vain endued him with the hindquarters of the hippopotamus. I presume the others had jumped it; the Quaker, with abysmal flounderings, walked through and heaved himself to safety on the farther bank. It was the dividing of the ways. My friendly company turned aside as one man, and I was left with the world before me, and no guide save the hoof-marks in the grass. These presently led me to a road, on the other side of which was a bank, that was at once added to the Quaker's black list. The rain had again begun to fall heavily, and was soaking in about my elbows; I suddenly asked myself why, in Heaven's name, I should go any farther. No adequate reason occurred to me, and I turned in what I believed to be the direction of Drumcurran.

I rode on for possibly two or three miles without seeing a human being until, from the top of a hill, I descried a solitary lady rider. I started in pursuit. The rain kept blurring my eyeglass, but it seemed to me that the rider was a schoolgirl with her hair hanging down her back, and that her horse was a trifle lame. I pressed on to ask my way, and discovered that I had been privileged to overtake no less a person than Miss Bobbie Bennett.

My question as to the route led to information of a varied character. Miss Bennett was going that way herself; her mare had given her what she called 'a toss and a half', whereby she had strained her arm and the mare her shoulder, her habit had been torn, and she had lost all her hairpins.

'I'm an awful object,' she concluded; 'my hair's the plague of my life out hunting! I declare I wish to goodness I was bald!'

I struggled to the level of the occasion with an appropriate protest. She had really very brilliant grey eyes, and her complexion was undeniable. Philippa has since explained to me that it is a mere male fallacy that any woman can look well with her hair down her back, but I have always maintained that Miss Bobbie Bennett, with the rain glistening on her dark tresses, looked uncommonly well.

'I shall never get it dry for the dance tonight,' she complained.

'I wish I could help you,' said I.

'Perhaps you've got a hairpin or two about you!' she said, with a glance that had certainly done great execution before now.

I disclaimed the possession of any such tokens, but volunteered to go and look for some at a neighbouring cottage.

The cottage door was shut, and my knockings were answered by a stupefied-looking elderly man. Conscious of my own absurdity, I asked him if he had any hairpins.

'I didn't see a hare this week!' he responded in a slow bellow.

'Hairpins!' I roared; 'has your wife any hairpins?'

'She has not.' Then, as an afterthought, 'She's dead these ten years.'

At this point a young woman emerged from the cottage and, with many coy grins, plucked from her own head some half-dozen hairpins, crooked and grey with age, but still hairpins, and as such well worth my shilling. I returned with my spoil to Miss Bennett, only to be confronted with a a fresh difficulty. The arm that she had strained was too stiff to raise to her head.

Miss Bobbie turned her handsome eyes upon me. 'It's no use,' she said plaintively, 'I can't do it!'

I looked up and down the road; there was no one in sight. I offered to do it for her.

Miss Bennet's hair was long, thick and soft; it was also slippery with rain. I twisted it conscientiously, as if it were a hay rope, until Miss Bennett, with an irrepressible shriek, told me it would break off. I coiled the rope with some success, and proceeded to nail it to her head with the hairpins. At all the most critical points, one, if not both, of the horses moved; hairpins were driven home into Miss Bennett's skull, and were with difficulty plucked forth again; in fact, a more harrowing performance can hardly be imagined, but Miss Bennet bore it with the heroism of a pin-cushion.

I was putting the finishing touches to the coiffure when some sound made me look round, and I beheld at a distance of some fifty yards the entire hunt, approaching us at a foot-pace. I lost my head, and instead of continuing my task, I dropped the last hairpin as if it were red-hot and kicked the Quaker away to the far side of the road, thus, if it were possible, giving the position away a shade more generously.

There were fifteen riders in the group that overtook us, and fourteen of them, including the Whip, were grinning from ear to ear; the fifteenth was Mr Tomsy Flood, and he showed no sign of appreciation. He shoved his horse past me and up to Miss Bennet, his red moustache bristling, truculence in every outline of his heavy shoulders. His green coat was muddy, and his hat had a cave in it. Things had apparently gone ill with him.

Flurry's witticisms held out for about two miles and a half; I do not give them, because they were not amusing, but they all dealt ultimately with the animosity that I, in common with himself, should henceforth have to fear from Mr Flood.

'Oh, he's a holy terror!' he said conclusively; 'he was riding the tails off the hounds today to best me. He was near killing me twice. We had some words about it, I can tell you. I very near took my whip to him. Such a bull-rider of a fellow I never saw! He wouldn't so much as stop to catch Bobbie Bennet's horse when I picked her up, he was riding so jealous. His own girl, mind you! And such a crumpler as she got too! I declare she knocked a groan out of the road when she struck it!'

'She doesn't seem so much hurt?' I said.

'Hurt!' said Flurry, flicking casually at a hound. 'You couldn't hurt that one unless you took a hatchet to her!'

The rain had reached a pitch that put further hunting out

of the question, and we bumped home at that intolerable pace known as a 'hound's jog'. I spent the remainder of the afternoon over a fire in my bedroom in the Royal Hotel, Drumcurran, official letters to write having mercifully provided me with an excuse for seclusion, while the bar and the billiard-room hummed below, and the Quaker's three-cornered gallop wreaked its inevitable revenge upon my person. As this process continued, and I became proportionately embittered, I asked myself, not for the first time, what Philippa would say when introduced to my present circle of acquaintances.

iii

'Your wife is extremely pretty,' pronounced Lady Knox autocratically, surveying Philippa between the candle shades; 'does she ride?'

'I'm glad you like her looks,' I replied, 'as I fear you will find her thoroughly despicable otherwise; for one thing, she not only can't ride, but she believes that I can!'

'Oh come, you're not as bad as all that!' my hostess was good enough to say; 'I'm going to put you up on Sorcerer tomorrow, and we'll see you at the top of the hunt—if there is one. That young Knox hasn't a notion how to draw these woods.'

iv

Lady Knox, square and solid, on her big, confidential iron-grey, was near me, and her eyes were on me and my mount; with her rubicund face and white collar she was more than ever like a coachman.

'Sorcerer looks as if he suited you well,' she said, after a few minutes of silence, during which the hounds rustled and cracked steadily through the laurels; 'he's a little high on the leg, and so are you, you know, so you show each other off.'

Sorcerer was standing like a rock, with his good-looking head in the air and his eyes fastened on the covert. His manners, so far, had been those of a perfect gentleman, and were in marked contrast to those of Miss Sally's cob, who was sidling, hopping and snatching unappeasably at his bit. Philippa had disappeared from view down the avenue ahead. The fog was melting, and the sun threw long blades of light through the trees; everything was quiet, and in the distance the curtained windows of the house marked the warm repose of Sir Valentine, and those of the party who shared his view of cubbing.

'Hark! hark to cry there!'

It was Flurry's voice, away at the other side of the covert. The rustling and brushing through the laurels became more vehement, then passed out of hearing.

'He never will leave his hounds alone,' said Lady Knox disapprovingly.

Miss Sally and the Cockatoo moved away in a series of heraldic capers towards the end of the laurel plantation, and at the same moment I saw Philippa on her bicycle shoot into view on the drive ahead of us.

'I've seen a fox!' she screamed, white with what I believe to have been personal terror, though she says it was excitement. 'It passed quite close to me!'

'What way did he go?' bellowed a voice which I recognized as Dr Hickey's, somewhere in the deep of the laurels.

'Down the drive!' returned Philippa, with a pea-hen quality in her tones with which I was quite unacquainted.

An electrifying screech of 'Gone away!' was projected from the laurels by Dr Hickey.

'Gone away!' chanted Flurry's horn at the top of the covert.

'This is what he calls cubbing!' said Lady Knox. 'A mere farce!' but none the less she loosed her sedate monster into a canter.

Sorcerer got his hind-legs under him, and hardened his

crest against the bit, as we all hustled along the drive after the flying figure of my wife. I knew very little about horses, but I realized that even with the hounds tumbling hysterically out of the covert, and the Cockatoo kicking the gravel into his face, Sorcerer comported himself with the manners of the best society. Up a side road I saw Flurry Knox opening half of a gate and cramming through it; in a moment we also had crammed through, and the turf of a pasture field was under our feet. Dr Hickey leaned forward and took hold of his horse; I did likewise, with the trifling difference that my horse took hold of me, and I steered for Flurry Knox with single-hearted purpose, the hounds, already a field ahead, being merely an exciting and noisy accompaniment of this endeavour. A heavy stone wall was the first occurrence of note. Flurry chose a place where the top was loose, and his clumsy-looking brown mare changed feet on the rattling stones like a fairy. Sorcerer came at it, tense and collected as a bow at full stretch, and sailed steeply into the air; I saw the wall far beneath me, with an unsuspected ditch on the far side, and I felt my hat following me at the full stretch of its guard as we swept over it; then, with a long slant, we descended to earth some sixteen feet from where we had left it, and I was possessor of the gratifying fact that I had achieved a good-sized 'fly', and had not perceptibly moved in my saddle. Subsequent disillusioning experience has taught me that but few horses jump like Sorcerer, so gallantly, so sympathetically, and with such supreme mastery of the subject; but none the less the enthusiasm that he imparted to me has never been extinguished, and the October morning ride revealed to me the unsuspected intoxication of fox-hunting.

Behind me I heard the scrabbling of the Cockatoo's little hoofs among the loose stones, and Lady Knox, galloping on my left, jerked a maternal chin over her shoulder to mark her daughter's progress. For my part, had there been an entire circus behind me, I was far too much occupied with

ramming on my hat and trying to hold Sorcerer, to have
looked round, and all my spare faculties were devoted to
steering for Flurry, who had taken a right-handed turn, and
was at that moment surmounting a bank of uncertain and
briary aspect. I surmounted it also, with a swiftness and
simplicity for which the Quaker's methods of bank jumping
had not prepared me, and two or three fields, traversed at
the same steeplechase pace, brought us to a road and to an
abrupt check. There, suddenly, were the hounds, scrambling
in baffled silence down into the road from the opposite
bank, to look for the line they had overrun, and there,
amazingly, was Philippa, engaged in excited converse with
several men with spades over their shoulders.

'Did ye see the fox, boys?' shouted Flurry, addressing the
group.

'We did! We did!' cried my wife and her friends in
chorus, 'He ran up the road!'

'We'd be badly off without Mrs Yeates!' said Flurry, as he
whirled his mare round and clattered up the road with a
hustle of hounds after him.

It occurred to me as forcibly as any mere earthly thing
can occur to those who are wrapped in the sublimities of a
run, that, for a young woman who had never before seen a
fox out of a cage at the Zoo, Philippa was taking to hunting
most kindly. Her cheeks were a most brilliant pink, her blue
eyes shone.

'Oh, Sinclair!' she exclaimed, 'they say he's going for
Aussolas, and there's a road I can ride all the way!'

'Ye can, miss! Sure we'll show you!' chorused her
cortége.

Her foot was on the pedal ready to mount. Decidedly my
wife was in no need of assistance from me.

Up the road a hound gave a yelp of discovery, and flung
himself over a stile into the fields; the rest of the pack went
squealing and jostling after him, and I followed Flurry over
one of those infinitely varied erections, pleasantly termed

'gaps' in Ireland. On this occasion the gap was made of three razor-edged slabs of slate leaning against an iron bar, and Sorcerer conveyed to me his thorough knowledge of the matter by a lift of his hindquarters that made me feel as if I were being skilfully kicked downstairs. To what extent I looked it, I cannot say, nor providentially can Philippa, as she had already started. I only know that undeserved good luck restored to me my stirrup before Sorcerer got away with me in the next field.

What followed was, I am told, a very fast fifteen minutes; for me time was not; the empty fields rushed past uncounted, fences came and went in a flash, while the wind sang in my ears, and the dazzle of the early sun was in my eyes. I saw the hounds occasionally, sometimes pouring over a green bank, as the charging breaker lifts and flings itself, sometimes driving across a field, as the white tongues of foam slide racing over the sand; and always ahead of me was Flurry Knox, going as a man goes who knows his country, who knows his horse, and whose heart is wholly and absolutely in the right place.

Do what I would, Sorcerer's implacable stride carried me closer and closer to the brown mare, till, as I thundered down the slope of a long field, I was not twenty yards behind Flurry. Sorcerer had stiffened his neck to iron, and to slow him down was beyond me; but I fought his head away to the right, and found myself coming hard and steady at a stone-faced bank with broken ground in front of it. Flurry bore away to the left, shouting something I did not understand. That Sorcerer shortened his stride at the right moment was entirely due to his own judgement; standing well away from the jump, he rose like a stag out of the tussocky ground, and as he swung my twelve stone six into the air the obstacle revealed itself as consisting not of one bank but of two, and between the two lay a deep grassy lane, half-choked with furze. I have often been asked to state the width of the boreen, and can only reply that in my opinion it was at least eighteen feet; Flurry Knox and Dr Hickey, who did not jump it, say that it is not more than five. What Sorcerer did with it I cannot say; the sensation was of a towering flight with a kick-back in it, a biggish drop, and a landing on cee-springs, still on the downhill grade. That was how one of the best horses in Ireland took one of Ireland's most ignorant riders over a very nasty place.

(From *Some Experiences of an Irish R. M.*)

An Irish Hunt

BY MARIGOLD ARMITAGE

ON this day, at this time, over this piece of country, Mike's theory about good scenting conditions seemed to be right. Hounds were racing, flinging, driving forward like a dappled cloud. There they went, over the great ditch, leaping, falling short, splashing, scrambling out and on without pausing to shake themselves. There went old George on his neat, wise horse, jumping cleverly, not an inch too far, not a second too soon, his ears cocked. Then Gillian, gloriously leading the field, going at it wildly. I knew that in the last second before the take-off, an expression of ecstatic agony upon her face, she would shut her eyes and hang tightly on to a plait of mane, leaving the reins to flap loose, and I was glad that Jane's mare knew her business. Then Tommy Dwyer, still crying encouragement to the tail hound, now streaking just behind old George, a personification of silent, bitter determination to catch up with the pack. Then it was my turn and the grey's stride never seemed to vary, only the dark water, the rushes fleeted suddenly backwards and were gone and he lowered his lean head as we met the steeply rising ground on the far side and his shoulder muscles worked like pistons beneath my knees. Now I was trying to control my wild excitement enough to think which would be the best line to take when we reached the top of the hill, where hounds were driving already over the low wall into the road. It was so long since I had hunted here that I had difficulty in visualizing the country. Once across the road there would be two or three fields, part of the point-to-point course, sloping gently towards Kilgarvan. But if they got him through the big covert would he swing right or left? On which flank of the pack should I station myself? And what the hell was the wind doing? It seemed to be blowing on my heated face from all directions at once. A snorting horse came up on my right hand. Father Carrigan tucked like a jockey behind its withers on a ragged racing saddle, his eyes gleaming wildly, his spectacles crooked on his nose, his bowler on the back of his head. I sighed inwardly with relief, for Father Carrigan knew the mind of every fox in the country.

'Follow me now, Anthony,' he shouted exultantly. 'Sure, I know this felly, he wouldn't mind how many miles he'd run. If he can't go down in Kilgarvan he'll go across the bog and make for the hills.'

Here he cursed his horse startlingly as it bungled the tiny walls into and out of the road, and streaked away down the big field, half-turned in his saddle to shout advice to me still over his black-clad shoulder.

'Bear right now, Anthony. Follow me. We must jump McCarthy's double where it's sound.'

McCarthy's double was the biggest bank in the country. Once I had gone over it on my feet when I was a boy and it was like climbing a minor Alp. I had sprung over the deep wet ditch, alighted about a quarter way up, hauled myself by grass-tuft and root and bramble on to the wide top where there was a beaten path amongst bushes and small trees, crept nervously half-way down the far side and then jumped unsuccessfully out over the six-foot stream and failed to clear it. I had got very wet and Nanny had lectured me.

In the middle of the field, cleared and reinforced, this bank was the official double of the point-to-point course—an enormous, smooth, green hummock, tempting you to jump it and carefully wired up to prevent just such goings-on. In some other places it was unsound, but Father Carrigan would know exactly where to have it. I took a pull and looked for Gillian. She was bearing away left, the silly piece, going down into Kilgarvan with old George and Tommy Dwyer, and she would certainly get lost and left and probably bogged. I yelled despairingly at her and waved furiously, and at last she saw me, hesitated, pulled round and came galloping over to me.

'Follow me, you silly woman. Follow Father Carrigan.'

We fled together down the gentle slope.

'Jump this exactly where he does. Look—there he goes.'

'*Jump this?*'

'Just leave it to the mare.'

'Oh—it's too easy.'

'Of course it is. You go first. I'll push you off the top if you stick.'

'Oh God—why did I *ever* imagine I was an outdoor girl?'

She shut her eyes.

The mare knew exactly what to do and she did it very slowly and deliberately. She looked at the ditch and decided the bottom was sound and waded slowly into it. 'No heroics for me,' her behind expressed to my horse, who was dancing with impatience. She then reared herself straight up with a wallowing noise, like a sea-monster, and arrived at the top of the bank in two heaving bounds which slightly loosened

Gillian, even though she had a different plait in each hand. They disappeared from my view and there was a series of sliding sounds and then a heavy thump. I could not see them, but I knew exactly what the mare had done. She had clambered carefully half-way down, just as I had done on my feet, and had then paused, waving her head and neck at the stream like an elephant testing something with its trunk, and shifting her hind-legs carefully to see of she had a firm take-off, while Gillian crouched nervelessly in her saddle with popping eyes, swallowing. Then she had jumped out and over it, just far enough and no farther.

'Are you out of the way?' I shouted.

A faint, wordless shriek of assent came back to me. Just as the grey started at it I was aware of Mike Harrington on his chestnut coming as if he was going into the last at Sandown and I thought, 'They'll both be killed without a doubt.' Then the grey was up and changing and over and out with a wonderful feeling of freedom and ease and effortless timing, so that for a second I saw myself on him, as Aunt Emmy did, 'tipping the double like a Punchestown horse' leading the field in the Hunt Cup—but only for a second.

Hounds were chiming away confidently down in Kilgarvan, and were obviously running hard through it. Father Carrigan had disappeared from my view but Gillian was galloping down the field in a determined manner that indicated she knew where he had gone. I set off after her, glancing uneasily back over my shoulder—for Mike was obviously going to be on the ground in a minute and supposing there was nobody else coming that way to pick him up? I wrestled unhappily with my conscience and the grey horse raked angrily at my uncertain hands and said, 'For God's sake let's *go*.' And then Mike and his chestnut appeared behind us, apparently soaring down from the sky, and turned a complete somersault before they hit the ground.

I very much regret having to record that my sole feeling

as I pulled my horse round was one of fury. I was going to miss what looked like an excellent hunt because Mike chose to ride a crazy racehorse over a country where what was needed was a cross between a pony and a panther. As I trotted back to them the horse thrashed uncertainly to its feet, looked round vaguely, saw Gillian's mare and made off down the field at full gallop, inextricably entangled in its reins. But Mike remained on the ground. And then like an answer to prayer, something altogether too good to be true, O excellent, cosy, capable, self-sacrificing man, Dr Paddy Herlihy from Garnagarry came slipping down off the bank on Mick O'Conner's pony that drew a cart to the creamery when it wasn't hunting.

He pulled up and dismounted in sad resignation, his pug-like face puckered.

'Couldn't I see what would happen a field away? Not the thrack of a heel did the horse lay to it, only knocked back at it with his tail—was it hurdling, God help us, he thought he was at? And I to have my first hunt for a fortnight, with the 'flu that's about.'

I hovered helpfully, and he looked up at me, from where he was poking gently at Mike, and grinned.

'Get away on to them, then you. What good that we'd both miss it? Sure, he's only winded and there's a dozen fellys about with dogs that can help me instead of confusing the hunt.'

With enormous relief and a certain amount of shame I hustled the willing grey off down the field. At the bottom was a sticky gap jammed with thorny bushes. I jumped it and heard hounds very close and swung right through an open gateway and there were Gillian and Father Carrigan, that first-class reader of foxy minds, breathing heavily and trying to hold their shifting horses still, while fifty yards away hounds went streaming and singing across the field in front of us.

'Oh, oh,' said Gillian to me, with shining eyes, her stock

under one ear and both leathers twisted where she had lost her irons over the double and jammed her feet back into them in a carefree manner.

'Didn't I tell you,' shouted Father Carrigan triumphantly. 'Sharp right he turned out of Kilgarvan and he's for the hills this minute.'

'Have you seen Brigadier Harrington's horse?' I asked him.

'I have, and he wouldn't let us lay a finger on him—he's gone into McCarthy's yearlings below—sure, McCarthy'll catch him when he'd settle.'

'Have you seen Mike?' Gillian asked me.

'I have, indeed, and the doctor from Garnagarry is with him now.'

'Oh, poor Mike—is he all right?'

'Not very.'

'Oh, Anthony, how can you be so heartless?'

'I feel like a character in Nimrod—the pace was too good to inquire. Come on, now.'

For old George had gone by, scrubbing his wise horse that wouldn't gallop unless the necessity was stark, and Tommy Dwyer had gone by with a purple, intent face and as we set off again two or three toiling figures were coming up from Kilgarvan—I looked back and thought I saw Hubert and the roan mare, Jane Harrington and a couple of unidentifiable forms behind them.

'Where's Andrew?' I shouted to Gillian as we galloped along the rutty headland with Father Carrigan, all rebounding off each other from time to time in a not very controlled manner. Her answer which seemed to contain the words 'little brute' was lost to me in the confusion that ensued at the next gap, where Father Carrigan's horse, who was slightly leading as we came to it, resolutely refused to jump a timber rail jammed across it that could not have been much more than eighteen inches high, coming to a jarring halt with a swerve that sent its rider down its shoulder. Gillian always said afterwards that she had heaved him back into the saddle by his respectable black breeches, but all I can remember is Father Carrigan pulling out of our way with a despairing cry of 'Holy God!' and sending his now willing horse scrambling over the bank, which was about twelve feet high, very narrow, extremely slippery and crowned with jagged, broken tree-stumps.

I reflected, as I looked back at him, on what a pity it was that his horse and Mike's could not somehow manage to combine their respective talents.

We pounded on. The banks were becoming wide, low, slippery humps, with big ditches full of water—we were approaching the bog. Here we would cross it at its narrowest part—about a mile—and then if we were lucky find ourselves in an excellent part of the country; grazing grounds with big, sound banks and small walls. 'The hills' which Father Carrigan had referred to was really *a* hill—Slievemore, the big blue shoulder rising out of the plain, with the dark, shifting cloud-shadows fleeting across its bulk, and the low, ragged clouds themselves lying now across its peak in banks which the freshening wind was beginning to blow away.

'See where he's making for,' I called to Gillian.

'If only I could breathe,' was her response, the brown mare plugging determinedly on beside me, her head low, delighted with her breathless and light and unmasterful rider, and confident in her own power to get there, wherever it might be. Behind us came Father Carrigan, still bitterly lecturing his non-timber-jumper, and behind him, apparently, still no one else at all. We pulled to a walk to slide down an extremely steep, short slope, at the bottom of which we would jump a huddle of stones, pretending to be a wall, and find ourselves on the bog road.

'Are we leading the field?' gasped Gillian as we slithered down towards it.

'Pounded 'em.'

'Oh . . . *fascinating.* . . . Do I look at all like Dick Christian?'

'Not really.'

'Oh. . . . I so hoped I did . . . I've never done such a thing before.'

Hounds went fleeting like a blizzard across the bog, old George and Tommy Dywer battering at a shameless gallop up the road after them.

'Oh,' said Gillian, as we landed together on to it, 'their poor glass legs will never stand it.'

I thought it more than probable. But there was nothing else to be done. There was goat-nibbled turf at the sides of the road, but there were deep, irregular ditches cut into it at frequent intervals, tiring and dangerous to horse and rider. Anyone who has tried to gallop a horse on a grass verge will know what a great penchant they have for the hard, high road in spite of their poor glass legs, and how they will bend and lurch and pull sideways towards it, refusing to look where they are going until they get their way, and the unique sensation of galloping on a hard, clattering surface.

'Anyway, it's not slippery,' said Gillian hopefully, as we fled along scattering stones, lurching in and out of ruts and making a noise like a hundred Crusaders charging in armour, 'but I couldn't feel guiltier, could you?'

Certainly I couldn't. Would the grey horse, I wondered, be lamed for life? But still the pace was too good to inquire. We must gallop or hounds would run away from us, so we galloped, guilty or not.

There was a broken-down cabin a little way on and from out of it slipped two lurchers, oblivious of shouted curses from within, to race, shrieking and nipping at the heels of old George's horse who, endeavouring to kick back at them as it galloped, very nearly came down. Old George's scream of execration and the pistol-cracks of his and Tommy Dwyer's thongs sent them howling and cowering into the ditch, from where they launched a further attack on us, while at the same time two apparently idiot children ran

gaily out under our horses' feet. Their mother, incredibly
tangled-looking and quite oblivious to their fate, hung over
the half-door of their home and screamed harshly, hadn't she
seen the fox himself and the dogs too ahead of us and they
never stopping to draw breath?

Neither did we draw breath, not then or for some time
after. It was a fearful moment. I shall never know exactly
what the grey horse did, but he managed somehow not to lay
the thrack of a heel on those undeserving brats—presumably
he knocked back at them with his tail. Gillian's mare
appeared to rise straight into the air in a sort of confused
fouetté—her feet working on nothing. Then we were past.

'I can't look back,' chattered Gillian.

I did so, with dread. The children, undismayed, were just
jumping gaily under Father Carrigan's horse—who became
so unnerved and so muddled with its feet that it ended up
wallowing in the ditch, with the lurchers in hysterics around
it. Benediction flowed from the father in an unending stream
as they struggled out again. Gillian always swore that he had
laid about the children with his whip, but I am ready to
believe that this was artistic license on her part, for Father
Carrigan, wild though he might be in appearance and be-
haviour, was the soul of kindness.

Now he came clattering on again behind us, talking angrily
to himself and suddenly behind him again there was an eager
hooting and, looking back, I saw my mother remorselessly
driving the groaning little green car with Richmond hanging
out of the window as if chasing gangsters in a rather bad
film. On one step clung somebody in pink (Mike? Colonel
Wilbraham? The Pytchley?) and on the other—could it be?
—it surely must be the tangled and unmaternal figure from
the cabin. Around the back wheels the indefatigable
lurchers nipped and shrieked once again, and farther back,
running nobly but rather hopelessly, wreathed in smelly
clouds from the exhaust came the abandoned children. And
then, far, far behind, just coming down on to the road, four

or six or so more conventional figures, correctly mounted and no doubt absolutely furious.

The grey cannoned heavily off Gillian's mare.

'Oh, do, *do* look where you're going, Anthony.'

'Oh, Lord,' I said, bending on the grey's neck.

'You're ill!' said Gillian, pallidly.

'No. But I've just seen Mama and Richmond with that terrible woman from the cabin.'

'Where? Where?'

'Not very far behind us.'

'I *can't* look. I daren't. If I start laughing now I'm finished.' She stared desperately ahead with a fixed face.

We were coming off the bog. The road was ceasing to have the appearance of a causeway and was tending to sink between thorn-crowned banks and become a boreen. We could hear hounds off on our left and bearing away.

'We must get out of here at the next jumpable place,' I said to Gillian.

Then we turned a sharp, downhill corner and fell slap on to old George and Tommy Dwyer, who were penned up facing an enormous, enthralled horse who was drawing a cart that just fitted the boreen. A small boy gesticulated helplessly from where he was sitting on the near shaft.

'Back,' roared old George at him in a Jehovah voice. 'Back, damn it, *back*!'

The boy stood up obediently and leaned heavily on the reins with the whole weight of his meagre body. The horse opened its mouth very wide, stuck its neck straight out and advanced towards us with an eager, welcoming sound.

'Dear heaven!' said old George hoarsely.

'Oh, *darling*,' said Gillian to me with tears in her eyes. '*Do* something. Make a hole in that.'

'That' was the high and healthy growth of blackthorn that crowned the bank on our left. The bank itself was not very high, but it looked slippery and rotten and the take-off out of the boreen was appalling.

'And the grandest gate you ever saw only just down from us!' wailed Tommy Dwyer.

He backed his horse and turned and booted him into the bank. Both were game but the thorns made a quick, clean jump impossible and as the horse dwelt the bank gave way immediately under his floundering feet. For a long few seconds he thrashed like a stranded whale above us. He was going to fall, but would he fall over or back into the lane? Tommy had slipped neatly off his back and was perched, like an anxious robin among the thorns, clutching the end of the reins. The horse gave one final desperate kick and disappeared from our view, sliding on his stomach. Tommy leapt after him into space. There was a hideous squelching sound.

'They'll be into the boggy dyke beyond for sure,' the small boy remarked conversationally.

Old George gave him a brimstone look. Suddenly the boy's face became illuminated with an idea.

'Wait while I run down and get the slasher for you.'

He leapt up and disappeared down the boreen. The abandoned horse and cart moved farther into the fearful mêlée.

'Tommy, are you clear, damn you?' bawled old George.

'Wait now, wait, sir.'

There were flounderings, and urging noises and then the encouraging cry, 'Come on now sir, but sure 'tis a grave you have to lep, 'tis a fearful place altogether.'

Old George set his purple jaw and lepped. I hung desperately on to the cart-horse, who had a strong notion of lepping himself.

Old George and his horse went the same way as Tommy and his—with the difference that old George was not spry enough to nip off. They rolled together out of sight.

'He'll be killed,' said Gillian, faintly. 'Why do we like doing this?'

Crash. Flounder. Squelch. And then a slightly shaken bawl: 'Come on then, you two.'

I wrestled strongly with the cart-horse.

'Listen, Gillian, don't have it. It's an awful place. Give it up.'

I felt a sharp panic for her, she looked so small suddenly. Her lips folded obstinately. Apparently she was still feeling like Dick Christian. The brown mare cocked her ears and seemed to take a deep breath.

They had it, determinedly. Old George said afterwards that even at that flustering moment, with his hounds running away from him every second, with his own horse still on the ground trying to get its breath back, with the winded Tommy Dwyer's whole weight on him as he tried to put him up; even so he was struck to stone by the sight of Gillian's arrival. She came with her eyes shut. She had abandoned her reins altogether and clung tightly with both hands to the pommel of her saddle. The mare made a wonderful effort, hit the edge of the 'grave' and tipped up. She ploughed on her head for a few yards and then righted herself, blowing mud triumphantly from her nostrils, with her bridle on the ground and her rider still in the saddle.

'I declare to my God,' Tommy Dwyer was wont to say in describing this feat afterwards, which he did very often, 'there's not a jock in the country, no not J. J. himself, would have stayed above the way Mrs Lodwick did, and the mare walking on her head the way she might be in a circus.'

But now it was my turn and the grey's. The expression 'riding for a fall' is very easily used and has a dashing ring about it—actually to do such a thing, however, arouses a feeling of sick anticipation comparable only to that experienced at the moment when the dentist's hand reaches for the drill.

We were not only going to fall, I felt, but there was also nothing to prevent the horse and cart from falling on top of us, since the horse was obviously feeling ambitious and there was no one to curb his feelings once I had gone. I belaboured him rather hopelessly with my whip until he gave way sufficiently to allow us a little room. My heart and stomach had changed places as the grey heaved himself up into the thorny gap, with everything giving way at once under his clever feet. But I need not have worried. The grey had brains and he decided instantly that, with no firm take-off, any attempt to jump the boggy dyke beyond would end in failure. Instead he dropped lightly and neatly and deliberately down into it and heaved himself out again, light and neat still, and shook himself with a noise like thunder all over old George's horse, which at once got to its feet indignantly.

'By heaven, that's a clever horse,' said old George. 'Mine just lost its head.'

He was clasping Gillian's mare's naked face delicately to his chest by nose and ear while Tommy Dwyer endeavoured to pick up her bridle, much hampered by his horse who had decided that the bridle was alive, and was refusing to go near it. I jumped off and took his horse and old George's while they restored to Gillian a measure of control and then I put them both up, and by that time I was so breathless with fright and exhaustion that I really thought I should lose the hunt yet through sheer physical inability to get up on the grey again. But Tommy Dwyer leant from his saddle and heaved nobly and I was aboard again and flying, for the grey had breathed himself nicely—there was agonizing mud in my right eye and I could not find my irons for a moment but ahead was good grass and sound banks—and behind a piteous, lonely, beseeching scream. I looked back. The cart-horse stood reared up with his forefeet on the bank, imploring us to return.

We fled on, through two delicious gateways without gates.

'Where's Father Carrigan?' Gillian shouted breathlessly.

Where indeed? I had forgotten him. I looked back. Nobody. He had been close behind us coming off the bog, and it was not like Father Carrigan to lose a good start.

Nor had he, for as I looked forward again, across the country that was now beginning to rise slightly as we went towards Sleivemore, there was the familiar crouched dark back, slipping along at least two fields ahead of us all.

'How did he get there?'

'Heaven knows.'

'That priest,' growled old George. 'He's always ahead of me, blast his Papist soul.'

Old George was well known never to have entered a church since he left Eton, but in the presence of Roman Catholicism his Protestantism was relentless and militant. He preferred, he said, his own type of damnation.

Old George's horse was tiring now; at the next bank he misjudged his distance and nearly fell back, Gillian's mare had a slight roll in her stride as we crossed the next field. I was frankly exhausted but the grey horse was going on as light as thistledown, his ears cocked still, still reaching for each jump eagerly, and I tried to sit as quiet as possible and not hinder him, even if I could not help him. There came a wall on to a cart-track, with a stone-faced bank out of it. Old George's horse came to his knees over the wall, slithered and scuffled and heaved and stopped with his chest against the bank, his head hanging over it and his tail stretched out, quivering.

'He's beat,' said old George. 'He's old, like me.'

He ran his hand lovingly down the wet shoulder.

'Get on to them, Tommy. What are you hanging about for?'

Tommy got on, with slither and slip and clatter, into a herd of young bullocks who wallowed excitedly with him down the field, ponderously playful.

'Get on, you two,' said old George. He had got off and was loosening his horse's girths, his head hidden under the saddle flap, so that his voice was muffled.

He didn't want us to see his face. I got off the grey and plucked George's reins from his hands.

'Get up, quick—he's a bottomless horse.'

Old George's face, taken from beneath the saddle flap, was even purpler than usual.

'I shouldn't do it to you, Anthony.'

'Don't be a fool.'

I pitched him up. My leathers were much too long—he crossed them over the pommel of the saddle and was gone, the grey jumping out big over the slight drop. Gillian looked woefully at me before she followed.

'Oh darling, the *chivalry*. Roger need never speak about Round Tables again.' Then she too was gone. There was the slap and thunder of their hooves and the bawling of the bullocks. Then silence, except for the heavy panting of old George's horse. Silence? Yes, silence. I strained my ears, but I could not hear hounds. And they had only been two or three fields ahead of us. A check? Had they overrun in this poached, bullock-foiled field? If so, there was hope for me yet. I turned the horse's head to the wind and earnestly exhorted him to breathe deeply which he did without hesitation. Then I heard Tommy Dwyer's voice not very far away raised in gentle encouragement to his hounds. Undoubtedly a check. And yet, what hope could there really be for me, since the fox was bound to be forward if he was making for Sleivemore? Or had he thought up something very tricky as he ran through the bullocks? I clambered to the top of the bank and looked about me. The field directly to the right of the one the bullocks were in ran increasingly boggily down to a narrow stream. Had he gone to cross it, the old customer, the cunning Charles James, running first in the middle of the bullocks and then turning sharply at a right angle off his point? If so, he would now be slipping at ease along the far bank, looking for a suitable place to re-cross it and point again for the haven of Sleivemore. As I cogitated and still no hound spoke, the little green car came roaring indomitably towards me and lurched to a standstill with its curious load.

'Anthony,' said my mother serenely, peering out at me. 'That's not Emmy's horse.'

'I know,' I said.

'Then where *is* Emmy's horse?'

Before I could answer there was another diversion—a clapping and flapping and thudding and a loose horse landing over the wall into our midst, wild-eyed, mud on its saddle, a leather gone and broken reins. My heart leapt up as I beheld it to be Conor Molloy's horse. It slithered up to old George's horse and blew on it in a friendly 'Thank-goodness-I've-found-someone-at-last' manner. Old George's horse laid its ears back and bit the newcomer smartly on the shoulder to show it its place.

'You hold this one,' said my mother sweetly to Richmond, pressing the broken rein into his hand with the air of someone distributing favours to the gentlemen at a charity ball. Richmond's hand closed, nervelessly, on it. He appeared to be speechless and was obviously strongly affected, but in what way I was not quite certain.

'Have the dogs the fox ate?' inquired the careless mother from the cabin.

'They have not, then,' I answered in the idiom.

'Where are they, Anthony? Oh, I forgot this is Colonel Bowser, he's staying with Poodle. (The Pytchley collar looked sharply defensive and fingered his stock.) And they're coming to have a drink with us tonight, that is, of course, if we can find her—or anyone—where *is* everyone, anyway?'

'All I know is that George has got Aunt Emmy's horse and he and Tommy and Gillian and Father Carrigan are over there—they seem to have checked and I think they probably overran it through those bullocks. I haven't seen anyone else at all, except as we came across the bog I thought perhaps I saw Jane and Poodle, a long way back.

'Nearly everybody went to the left around Kilgarvan, that's what happened and they got thrown out and they

haven't caught up yet.' She looked back over the wall.
'Here's somebody now.'

It was Caroline. The Araby little horse, black with sweat,
landed neatly and jauntily beside us and tossed its head
rudely at the other two. Caroline's smile was enchanting, her
face creamy under the mud-splashes, her velvet eyes glowing.

'Thank heaven I found somebody at last—I do hate
following hoof-marks. Where are they? Why have you got my
father's horse, Anthony?'

Oh, noble, pure and unselfish motive thus happily turned
to glorious gain! I explained.

'How *very* kind of you. Listen, I'll tell you what you can do.
Change bridles and get up on Conor's horse.'

'Oh yes, Anthony,' said my mother. 'You mustn't miss it
now.' She was already divesting George's horse of its bridle.
'Just take hold of an ear, would you, Mr Kerr. That's it, he
won't try and move.'

But he did. For at that very instant the ringing, the
clamour, broke again on the air and the triumphant twang-
ing of old George's horn. My thumb was in Conor's horse's
mouth as it mumbled angrily at the strange and frothy bit,
refusing to take it.

'Oh hurry, hurry,' wailed Caroline, in a frenzy. 'Oh,
listen to them, the darlings—hurry, hurry.'

Old George's horse, breathed and rid of the weight and
highly indignant at the strange turn of affairs, twitched his
ear away from Richmond, jumped the bank with a grunt and
was away, the saddle slowly sliding round under his belly as
he went.

'I told you to hold his ear, Mr Kerr,' said my mother
mildly. I twisted my thumb madly in Conor's horse's mouth,
jammed in the bit, pulled the bridle with an effort over his
ears—it was too tight for the poor brute—and left the
throat-latch dangling as Poodle's boy-friend bent to give me
a leg up; a noble lift that nearly sent me clean over the big

horse—the Pytchley back, I saw as he bent, was smeared with mud from collar to skirt.

I am very glad that there exists no photograph of myself jumping that bank on Conor's horse. I think my head was somewhere near his tail as we landed and I can remember seeing my hands raised in front of me as if in prayer. Then we were scudding away after Caroline and from somewhere not so very far ahead, once again unfaltering, the glorious voices came back to us.

I have no very clear recollection of the rest of the hunt. I realized at once that I had no hope of holding Conor's horse, who seemed to be as fresh as a daisy, and was taking delighted advantage of the mild half-moon snaffle that had replaced his own twisted one. He was big and awkward, green and hot, and his jumping was slapdash, to say the least of it. No thought of refusing ever entered his head, he went gaily and gallantly into his fences with his ears cocked, but with no very clear-cut idea as to what he was going to do about them. He had great panache, but all his decisions were made in mid-air. Twice he was nearly down—more times than I care to remember I was nearly off. I was riding without stirrups, since one is no good to anybody, and I was getting very tired. I gave him his head and prayed and once or twice adopted Gillian's expedient of shutting my eyes. We passed Caroline, who shouted something happily to me, we passed Father Carrigan, whose horse was reduced to a toiling jog, 'God help us, Anthony, what horse have you now?'

Half a field ahead Gillian's brown mare was doggedly cantering, rolling like the *Queen Mary* in a heavy sea, and ahead again, forging farther, jumping cleanly still, the game grey horse carried old George to his hounds.

The land was rising ever more steeply, the wide green fields, the sound banks giving way to rough, tussocky little enclosures, patchworked by little crumbling walls. Sleivemore, enormous in the fading light, bulked silent and close above us, shutting out the pallid evening sky. We were coming on to its lower slopes. At the next wall Gillian's mare's heels waved in the air, she tipped up and crumbled amongst the tussocky grass. I landed near them.

'Oh darling, *heavens*, what horse have you got now—did you see us fall?—do, *do* go on, quick. I'll just wait until this poor honey gets her breath—I see Father Carrigan coming—do, *do* go on.'

Now, as I went, I saw hounds again for the first time since we had crossed the bog, driving across a low ridge above and to the left of me. They had had a view, I thought, for the high screaming for blood had come into their voices. After them the grey horse slipped like a ghost. Conor's horse lowered his head to climb, picking his way on the rocky outcrop. We came up with Tommy Dwyer limping, leading his beaten horse, almost in tears.

'Sure, don't they deserve him, if hounds ever did? But he'll get into the rocks above and then he can run the whole inside of the hill—the bloody place is hollow—who'd ever think they'd bring him to here from Drumanagh?'

'Never mind, Tommy—it must be a twelve-mile point— you've given us all something to talk about.'

But Tommy was thinking of his hounds. Conor's horse slid and slithered.

'Best get off now, sir, 'tis a dreadful place for a tired horse.'

When I did so I went to my knees. My legs seemed to be made of cotton wool, and my feet to have no connection with the rest of me. I was not quite sure where I was putting them, and I staggered along drunkenly. Away in front, abruptly, the voices died. Then they clamoured again, but singly, brokenly, mournfully, informing us of frustration and a thirst unassuaged. Old George's horn told us the same, and round the spine of the ridge we came upon them, a little above us, milling and crying around the great earth in the rocks, the grey horse standing amongst them, his head drooping at last, and old George's face glowing like a lantern through the deepening dusk.

'By God, they nearly had him, the darlings, they were running right into him. Ten yards more, five even and he wouldn't have made it.'

'A good fox,' I said. 'A marvellous run, George. You've made history today. Congratulations.'

'And only the locals up,' said old George with immense satisfaction. 'Leave him, leave him now, my darlings. Count 'em, Tommy—I think they were all on.'

'Here comes one non-local,' I said, as Gillian came plodding up towards us, trailing Jane's mare, like a tired child dragging a balloon away from a party. Behind her came Caroline and Father Carrigan, both also on foot. Father Carrigan seemed to have caught old George's horse and was leading it by the thong of his whip looped round its throat. The old horse lifted his head and whinnied in a throaty murmur when he saw hounds.

We stood around idly, enveloped in an immense tiredness and content. Old George and Tommy were murmuring endearments to their lovely hounds as they counted them and pulled thorns out of sore pads.

There was a smell of sweating horses and the evening wind, and a star was out above Sleivemore. Old George put the horn to his lips for the last time and blew the long, heart-rending 'Home'.

(From *A Long Way to Go*)

The Baron and His Horse

ANON

My spirited Lithuanian had almost brought me into a scrape; I had an advanced forepost, and saw the enemy coming against me in a cloud of dust, which left me rather uncertain about their actual numbers and real intentions. To wrap myself up in a similar cloud was common prudence, but would not have much advanced my knowledge, or answered the end for which I had been sent out; therefore I let my flankers on both wings spread to the right and left, and make what dust they could, and I myself led on straight upon the enemy, to have a nearer sight of them. In this I was gratified, for they stood and fought till, for fear of my flankers, they began to move off rather disorderly. This was the moment to fall upon them with spirit; we broke them entirely —made a terrible havoc amongst them, and drove them not only back to a walled town in their rear, but even through it, contrary to our most sanguine expectation.

76

The swiftness of my Lithuanian enabled me to be foremost in the pursuit; and seeing the enemy fairly flying through the opposite gate, I thought it would be prudent to stop in the market-place to order the men to rendezvous. I stopped, gentlemen, but judge of my astonishment when in this market-place I saw not one of my hussars about me. Are they scouring the other streets, or what is become of them? They could not be far off, and must, at all events, soon join me. In that expectation I walked my panting Lithuanian to a spring in this market-place, and let him drink. He drank uncommonly, with an eagerness not to be satisfied, but natural enough, for when I looked round for my men, what should I see, gentlemen? the hind part of the poor creature— croup and legs were missing, as if he had been cut in two, and the water ran out as it came in, without refreshing or doing him any good! How it could have happened was quite a mystery to me, till I returned with him to the town gate. There I saw that when I rushed in pell-mell with the flying enemy they had dropped the portcullis (a heavy falling door, with sharp spike at the bottom, let down suddenly to prevent the entrance of an enemy into a fortified town) unperceived by me, which had totally cut off his hind part, that still lay quivering on the outside of the gate. It would have been an irreparable loss had not our farrier contrived to bring both parts together while hot. He sewed them up with sprigs and young shoots of laurel that were at hand; the wound healed, and, what could not have happened but to so glorious a horse, the sprigs took root in his body, grew up, and formed a bower over me, so that afterwards I could go upon many other expeditions in the shade of my own and my horse's laurels.

(From *The Travels of Baron Münchausen*)

Somewhere in France

BY RICHARD BALL

SUDDENLY the 'strafe' broke into being. A roaring shriek above their heads, a faraway bang, another and another.... The squadron commander glanced up from the book he had been reading.

Roger remembered the transport, perhaps already at Quality Corner, and his old favourite, Broncho, with Harry at the farm.

'Look here, you fellows,' he said, 'I'd better be going. My show must be half-way back by now, and it looks to be pretty hot just thereabouts.'

'Stay a bit, Arbuthnot, I'd advise you. It sounds pretty bad back there now. If they're in it they're in it, and if they're not they're not; and you can't do much good either way.'

'Still, sir, I ought to be with them, so I think I'd better have a try.'

The next moment he was running up the steps, into the noise and the screaming of the hurtling shells. Flash after flash lit up the night as he hurried along. The shells looked to be falling short of their objective, but very close to the derelict farm.

Figures rose out of the darkness and sank silently back again as he hurried on. The transport had passed him on their way back half an hour ago, one of the regimental police told him, and glanced in surprise after Roger as he hurried forward. Then, shrugging his shoulders, and muttering that he wouldn't 'give the young fellow half a chance', he turned to thoughts of his duty. Roger hurried on.

Some few shells had fallen about the reserve line as he came down the communication trench; now the range was increasing and they had crept up to the farm.

And Broncho was at the farm!

There was a lull in the shelling as at last he stopped out on to the road. It was still so dark that it was only with difficulty he found his way; but every now and then a flare momentarily lit up the landscape, showing him the farmhouse ruins in front. Thanking Providence for the lull, he hurried on; but as he reached the yard a shell landed in the orchard, raising a shower of clay and stones, to come pattering down about and around him. But the ruins of the house were still as they had been, and, flashing his torch as he hurried through the doorway, he saw Harry with the horses, restive but unharmed.

'Old man,' he whispered, as he led Broncho out, followed by Harry, and climbed into the saddle, 'we've got to face it together, you and I!'

As they picked their way through the debris another shell fell, short of them, then another far away in front, and a third as they turned up the road towards Quality Corner, and as Roger glanced back he saw the ruins of the house springing into flame behind him. The trot became a gallop. The burning farm lighted up the first stretches of the road. Shell after shell fell methodically—to the right, to the left, behind, in front. But they seemed in luck's way. Another half-mile and they would be at Quality Corner. There was no sign of the transport, so it looked as though it must have got through. Bending low in his saddle, Roger ran a hand along Broncho's neck.

'Steady, old man,' he whispered, 'we're leaving Harry behind, but we've nearly come through the worst of it.'

At that moment there came a roar and a sudden blinding flash.

The transport at last had reached the sanctuary of 'Longneck'. Old Evans, the quartermaster, was congratulating the sergeant on having come safely through as dirty a night as one could wish to see, when he caught the sound of a horse coming slowly down the village street.

'Cripes!' he said; 'here's young Roger back. He's all right, but where's Harry?'

But as the slow, limping horse with a figure crouched low over the pommel of the saddle turned into the lines he realized that it was not quite 'all right'. Evans ran forward. 'He's got one, he has! Come and catch hold of him, Bill,' he cried.

Carefully they lifted Roger down.

'Arm and shoulder, shell splinter,' announced the Quartermaster, running his hand over the sodden jacket. 'Broncho's got one too, Bill! What's his?'

'Same thing, far's I can see,' answered the other, after a moment's inspection. 'Poor brute, there's a big piece tore clean out.'

ii

Roger woke again to consciousness amid a smell of antiseptics and a sense of whiteness and much light. He would, he was told, be transferred to the base and thence to England.

Harry, lying pinned beneath his dead horse, had been picked up by some gunner soon after dawn. Broncho, he heard, in answer to his inquiries, was also being moved to the base. But no more information about his horse was vouchsafed him. In the words of the old *curé*, 'It was the war!'

Broncho had sunk exhausted when at length he had succeeded in hobbling back to the *curé's* stable on that eventful night, and the old man, coming to visit him early in the morning, had murmured sympathetically to Harry that it was the war. '*C'est la guerre, mon enfant! Hélas le beau cheval!*'

Shrapnel wounds, torn ligaments. Such was the official verdict upon Broncho's injuries. It depended—the veterinary officer did not state explicitly upon what—as to whether he would ever be quite well again . . . And so Broncho, his shoulder so numb and irresponsive that he could scarcely move, his seared flesh protected from infection by hurriedly applied dressing, was loaded with difficulty into a horse ambulance, and thus began the first stage of his journey down to the base. Pain and exhaustion were struggling for mastery in his spent frame as the ambulance jolted along. Sometimes his eyes were open, displaying the wide iris of pain. Sometimes for long periods they were closed, and his head leaned dejectedly against the side of the ambulance. But whenever he opened them the world throbbed and swam before him. And whenever they were closed that dull throbbing, and the dull grinding of the wheel along the pot-holed road, seemed to centre itself in his exhausted brain. Life passed him by mistily. Voices, faces, all were strange. Harry's pained face had passed from view as the ambulance lurched out of the *curé's* yard, and of his master there had been no sign since they had struggled home through the night together. Yet hands which, even in the midst of his exhaustion, he had recognized as skilful and tender had come to give him first aid in the *curé's* stable. Skilful hands, too, had aided him to struggle up the ambulance's sloping platform. And when at last they came to a stand, some two hours later, on the little quay beside the broad canal, those same skilful hands and soothing tones came to aid and encourage him in his climb down again.

A spring-time breeze came eastward up the long stretch of the canal, rippling the placid waters and causing the moored barges to rock gently against the walls of the quay. It came, too, that cool, spring-time breeze, to ruffle the matted forelock that hung upon Broncho's forehead, to cool his throbbing brain and wipe the mists of pain from before his eyes. And so, lifting his tired head, he glanced about him at the long stretch of rippling water, at the dark barges moored to the quay, and, lastly, at the long line of stricken horses—of which he himself was one—patiently waiting their turn to go on board. Slowly, painfully, the short journey to the gangway was accomplished. With difficulty they hobbled across one by one. Lowering his head, Broncho struggled into the improvised stall beneath the fluttering tarpaulins, skilful hands to aid his progress, encouraging voices to urge him on. And there, his quarters leaned against the rail, the rope of his halter hanging motionless beneath his chin, black exhaustion came down upon him once more. He knew nothing of the noisy waking to life of the barge's engine, or of its slow putting out, with its cargo of stricken, on to the placid water of the canal.

When he woke it was again daylight, but whether a day had passed or no he could not have told. Thirst had come upon him. His mouth was hot and dry, his tongue rough and clumsy; but water had been left by his side, from which he drank. There was feeding there too, a few handfuls of crushed oats mixed with bran, a bundle of forage tied to the rail of the standing—but he felt too sick to eat. And there he stood—dully conscious of the sounds around him, of the occasional stamping of his neighbour's feet, of the slow breeze flapping among the tarpaulins, of the vibration of the barge's engine and the faint wash of the placid waters against its bow, but far more so of that flaming pain which every now and again shot upward through his being, and of that dull throbbing which marked every movement, his head bent low as his spirit submitted, with animal patience, to endure.

Suddenly the spluttering of the engine died away. Slowly the barge drifted in once more to a quayside. And then, with a sound of gangways clattering into place, of newcomers hurrying on board, of orders being given and acknowledged, it was borne upon Broncho that he had reached one more stage on the way to his destination. Soon enough, too, came skilful hands to aid him in his progress to the shore. Blinking, stumbling, every breath a difficulty, every movement pain, he slowly made his way out into the sunlight.

'Operating theatre,' said a voice at his side, and the orderly at his head saluted. And then, hobbling painfully across the barrack square, he was led into a building where white-coated men were waiting to receive him.

'Shrapnel case, sir,' explained the lieutenant in charge.

A big man in a white coat nodded.

Broncho, sniffing a strange smell that hung in the air, saw that they were tying hobbles on his feet. What was it for, he wondered? Did they not know that he was prepared to bear whatever they wished to do to him, that he had learned from his master to trust men? A rope was quickly fastened round his body. A deft movement—and he was lying on the ground! Some of the old-time fire flashed in his eye as he tried to lift his head in protest. But then something came floating about his nostrils—something against which his senses were powerless to protest, and the next moment he was lying unconscious on the floor.

'Well,' said the surgeon, fitting his knives back into their case, 'I think I have made a good job of it. Look at that, and that, and that . . .' He nodded his head towards several rough-edged lumps of metal. 'I don't think there can be anything left. But as for the ligaments, it'll take them a long time to knit!'

Broncho, upon the floor, was slowly regaining consciousness. With half-opened eyes he watched the figures moving to
and fro.

'Gallant horse, too,' the big man continued, looking
down at him. 'I'd spare no pains to try to save him. I can't
think of another struggling so far with so much metal
inside.'

'Do you think he'll come right, sir?' his assistant questioned.

'Can't say yet. It's about an even-money chance.'

Twice a day for a long time after that the big man came
himself to see Broncho in his stall, to adjust strappings and
dress his wounds. And the touch of those fingers, so skilfully
soothing his pain, told Broncho that the big man was a
friend. Slowly but surely that jagged wound began to heal.
And one morning, as the big man bent absorbed over his
work, Broncho tried to make achnowledgement. Very
gently he turned his head and slowly rubbed his muzzle
against his shoulder.

'Steady, horse!' the latter murmured, intent on his work.

Again, Broncho tried, touching the stooping shoulder; and
this time the big man looked up and understood.

'Thanking me, are you? Well, if I *am* a good doctor, I
must say you are a good patient.' He smiled. 'Between us
we'll have you right again one day, old man.' He stood upright, looking above the orderly's head into Broncho's wise
eyes. 'And I'll bet you've got a bit of a history, too,' he
murmured.

iii

It was later, almost two years later—for a clear mid-
March dusk lingered as though loth to fall upon the level
countryside—when Broncho once more set forth with his
master upon an eventful journey, marching at the head of
the column along the Bapaume road. Roger, following the

familiar figure of Sir Charles, sat erect in his saddle, gazing out before him into the spring-time dusk. Ahead, in the distance beyond Péronne, from somewhere towards the heights of St Quentin, came the desultory rumbling of the guns. And along the shell-pitted road that led from Albert to Bapaume the Southshires hurried, to the clatter of hoofs and the jingle of bits. Roger, riding along at the head of his squadron, was very conscious of a feeling of foreboding, though why he could not have said. But he drew comfort from the thought that, now that at last the call for cavalry had come again, Broncho was with him once more to share that future that lay in that region of battle whence sounded the rumbling of guns.

In the lines beyond Ypres, war had lain her hands upon them both. And now they were again together. Roger, some three months after he had been wounded, had returned to his regiment, a shattered regiment, with Adams as second-in-command and Jimmy Smith as squadron commander. But Broncho's wounds had been more severe. All that first summer he had lain in the sick-lines. Autumn had come before he had begun to limp painfully about the exercising paddocks. And save that he had trusted in his friends, in the round-faced orderly—not unlike Harry—in the big surgeon with the gentle voice and the skilful hands, life had seemed very dreary until one day he had caught the sound of a long-remembered voice.

Long-remembered! It had been so very long since he had last heard it that it had almost faded into a memory of the past. Yet at its faintest echo that past sprang to life once again. His ears pricked eagerly forward. He gazed with a revived keenness in the direction whence it had come. And the next moment he caught sight of his master walking quickly towards him along the lines, by Roger's side the big surgeon in whose charge he was.

'Yes, sir,' Roger was explaining. 'He is the only horse I have ever owned. I bought him myself—had to save up a good bit to pay for him! Had him with me from the time that I came out until the day we were hit. . . .'

Then, with his hand resting upon Broncho's neck, he listened to the veterinary officer's explanation:

'A case of touch and go. . . . I think I may be proud of his recovery. Of course, it will be some time before he is fit again. But he's steadily improving. Broncho you said his name was, didn't you? Aren't you much better latterly, Broncho old man?'

And then Roger, running his fingers slowly over Broncho's temples with that motion which the latter had come to know and love, with a few whispered words had tried to thank his horse for all he had done for him on that night of long ago.

'I've got to thank you for a lot, old man! You struggled the whole way home. If you hadn't—well, most likely I shouldn't be here to talk of it today.'

'Struggled his way right back to the transport lines,' he explained to his companion. 'Can't think how he managed it—especially now you've told me how bad he was. And one thing, sir, I want you to remember please, that whenever he's fit again I want to get him back?'

The big man laughed.

'Oh, I'll remember! Broncho's a friend of mine, too. Where's this you say your regiment is—resting?'

'Yes, and likely to continue to, I should think,' answered Roger. 'They got a pretty good shaking after I got hit.'

And thus it was that, when now at length the call had come once again, Broncho was, with his master, ready to answer it.

They reached Bapaume an hour or so after nightfall, bivouacking to the south of the town. And among the gathering forces that had come hurrying up from Albert, southward from Arras and northward from Amiens, rumour ran rife. The German front lines were empty—so Roger was assured. The enemy had been retreating since the beginning of the week. . . .

'And if you ask me,' continued a Canadian who was one of Roger's many chance informants, 'it's the beginning of the end! They can't hold the line! They've been evacuating their heavy stuff for a month or more. . . . I've been out the last two days. Got as far as their second line, nothing to be found but fallen-in trenches! But the going's too heavy for us footsloggers. That's why they're bringing the cavalry up.'

Roger agreed, glancing beyond his informant at the broken black buildings of the town and at the stars that hung above in the spring-time sky. To him—and more especially at this moment—there was something mysterious about that vista of dark, twisted shapes against the paler sky of the night, and about the lights that came and went with muffled glow, and the darkness that hid the ordered movements of all those hastily gathered men.

'They tell me the Albert road was stiff with cavalry today?' The Canadian looked his question.

'We came up this afternoon,' answered Roger, 'and we're to move again at daybreak.'

'Well, good luck to you, old man—and good hunting!' And with a dry laugh the gaunt figure in the buttoned-up greatcoat swung off down the road.

Roger's glance followed him into the darkness. Then it returned to the indistinct shapes of the town that rose up huddled against the sky. And then, with a glance up at the flickering stars and a thought of what the morrow might hold, he turned back to his bivouac.

Jimmy was alone when he got there, studying the next day's plans. He glanced up with relief as Roger came through the doorway.

'Hullo!' he said, 'that you? These have been sent down. Come and have a look at them.'

Roger bent over his shoulder towards the table, moving the lantern back a little so that the light did not strike up into his eyes.

'Here we are,' explained Jimmy, his finger on the map. 'We're to start at daybreak. . . . Not to lose touch! Infantry following . . . and guns. . . .'

Roger nodded. It *did* seem, as the Canadian hinted, not unlike the end!

But Jimmy was not so optimistic—for he had grown severe and practical with the responsibility of war.

'We'll be up against their rearguard all the time,' he pointed out. 'The old man says his information is that about their lines will be very difficult going, but that once we get beyond them the country is untouched. I'll want you to lead the first patrol. Pick your men—and remember to go slow.'

Roger stood upright, with flushed face.

'Right, old man,' he said, 'and thanks!'

Jimmy glanced up at him questioningly from his rickety stool. Why the thanks, he wondered?

But to no one was Roger going to divulge his determination that Broncho should be the first horse to cross the line!

They set off at daybreak the next morning, skirting Bapaume and feeling their way steadily forward. Behind them followed infantry and guns.

All about them the country lay silent with a sinister peace, a silence broken only at time by the low rumble of the guns up north, where the enemy still stood his ground. Here they could yet find no target.

Sometimes from their right or left came distant sounds of rifle or machine-gun fire, but after a few minutes these would die away.

The day wore on. Mile after mile was covered, yet never an enemy was to be seen. Often Broncho, champing his bit with growing impatience, looked with longing at long stretches of down that were before him. Yet there was rarely ever a gallop, and then but for a short hundred yards or so when Roger pushed on in answer to the signals of one of his scouts ahead.

In the afternoon, men and horses tired alike, they turned

southwards a little where the Canal du Nord crossed their path, and Roger, with an impatience equal to Broncho's own, still continued to press onwards, under the influence of the hour that seemed to be urging them to advance and still advance! Then suddenly, through the failing light, a grey figure flitted across the road before him. The enemy? At last! Instantly, almost instinctively, he urged Broncho forward, subconsciously thinking to hear his men thunder up behind. But those grey figures he now saw through the trees were not hurrying in retreat. Fifty yards he rode—alone. Then, with a strange roaring in his ears, a sound of many waters, he swayed in his saddle and crashed blindly to the ground. The merest wisp of smoke drifted into nothingness above the muzzle of a German rifle. A moment or two later, dazed and helpless, he felt himself lifted up by enemy hands, and realized with a deep bitterness that he was a prisoner.

iv

Broncho, too, had seen that flitting grey form. His eyes, keener than his master's, had noted the 'enemy' crouching in the shadow of the trees. But to him, in that unsuspecting moment, the world had held no 'enemy', for, thanks to Roger's care and patience, his confidence in mankind had been regained. And then, out of the shadows, there had come that spurt of flame! Through the evening's stillness the sharp crack of a rifle had come to mock at horse and rider. One moment, Broncho had felt his master swaying in the saddle, clutching desperately at the reins. The next, Roger was lying on the ground, a crumpled heap, and he himself was tearing wildly back along the hillside road.

Down through the dusk he tore, terror lending wings to his feet. He had seen those grey figures, vindictive, triumphant, come leaping out of the shadow. And that glimpse of his master, in whom he so trusted, now huddled up in helplessness, that realization of the destruction wrought upon man by man, in one fell instant swept away every shred of that confidence which had so carefully been rebuilt. With a wild snort of terror he turned and tore away into the dusk—a maniac—his one object flight. . . .

The patrol were riding slowly up the hill, anxiously hoping to come into touch again with their leader. The rider-less horse tore through them round a bend in the road, finishing the tale that the sudden rifle-shot in the wood had begun. But even as they glanced round in their saddles at him in dismay he had disappeared once more into the dusk, hoof-beats echoing back feverishly through the night, his saddle flapping wildly against his sides as he fled on.

Mile after mile he tore on, swerving from every sound, his heart throbbing hardly beneath his ribs, his breath coming ever and ever more painfully, his hoofs beating more and more mechanically upon the muddy road. At length, after what seemed to his numbed senses like a lifetime, he realized that he could fly no farther. Gradually, unknown to him, his pace had grown slower and slower. At last, with a few heaving breaths, he had faltered into a walk, then to a stand, and at last—with head thrust forward and heaving flanks—stood spent and beaten in the darkness, no sound in his ears save the wild beating of his heart.

It was long afterwards that the chill of the spring-time night, penetrating his spent, sweat-drenched body, brought to his numbed senses some realization of his plight. He was alone, lost in a world of darkness, his every energy exhausted, at the mercy of the old enemy—Man!

The night chill, creeping ever deeper through his ex-hausted body, urged movement. Once, and then again, he faltered, his knees shaking beneath him when he tried to move. The third time, with an effort, he succeeded in hob-bling onward; but his shoulders had stiffened and his feet had grown leaden, and each step seemed to turn every muscle and sinew to a cord of red-hot flame. Yet instinct urged food and shelter. Feebly he tried to crop at the grass beneath his feet, but even that scant herbage seemed to stick in his parched throat. Water! He sniffed at the air, casting his head to left and right questioningly. But there was no water thereabouts that his dulled nostrils could sense. Shelter? A spring-time wind blew over the plateau, but there seemed to be no shelter from it that he could find. And so, spent, stained with sweat and mud, his broken reins trailing the ground about him, he hobbled aimlessly onward through the darkness of the night.

But at last there came a sound through the darkness, the sound of voices, close at hand! With a wild snort of terror Broncho sprang forward, blundering on through the dark. But the next moment something unseen tripped him up and he fell headlong, and, huddled upon the ground, knowing nothing of where he was or how he had come there, sank into complete unconsciousness.

Thus it was that Private Harris of the Lancashires, who in civil life had been in the textile trade, struggling sleepily from beneath the flap of his improvised tent into the mists of early morning, stumbled, in the half-light, across what he plaintively declaimed to be a 'bloomin' 'orse'.

The sergeant-major, following fussily in answer to his call, looked down in astonishment at Broncho's spent form, stretched stiffly no more than a yard or two beyond their bivouac.

'He weren't there last night, sergeant!' exclaimed Private Harris excitedly. 'That I'll go bail!'

'Officer's saddle horse!' quoth the sergeant in his best official manner. 'But there don't seem to be no rider?'

'There ain't any,' said Private Harris with conviction. 'He's just—loose. . . .'

'Saddled and bridled,' continued the sergeant, as though he were making an inventory.

'Strike me!' interrupted Bert Harris excitedly. 'He ain't dead after all! Look, he's opened his blinkin' eye!'

The sergeant moved pompously round.

'So he has,' he agreed, 'So he has.' He gazed down stolidly at Broncho, while Broncho, with returning consciousness, gazed blankly up at him. Then, feeling that the situation had grown beyond him, he cleared his throat long and fully. 'Well, anyhow, it ain't any of our business, young Harris,' he decided. 'We'd best be going our ways and leave it to them as it belongs to.'

Thus it was that, an hour or so later, young Tanner of the A.V.C. came busily along.

'Seen a dead horse, or a half-dead horse?' he queried.

'Yes, sir!' The sergeant saluted briskly. 'Just round to the right, sir.' And Bert Harris, behind him, jerked his thumb over his shoulder for the information of young Tanner's orderly, and nodded at the sergeant's back and slowly winked one eye.

Young Tanner strode rapidly round, and halted a pace or two from where Broncho lay. The mystery that had intrigued Bert Harris and puzzled the sergeant did not strike him. What his professional instincts allowed him to see was an utterly spent horse. He looked back at his following orderly. He then looked at the conformation of the ground. He fingered the humane destroyer in his tunic pocket.

'Could load him there quite easily,' he said to himself, 'so I suppose it would be most merciful to put a bullet through the poor brute.'

He came forward a pace. He bent down and drew slightly upward with his fingers the loose skin of Broncho's lip. He glanced at the swollen tongue. He bent his head and listened carefully to the faint beating of the horse's heart. 'Yes,' he decided, 'as well to put an end to him.' He turned and motioned the orderly to get the saddle and bridle off, and taking the destroyer out of his pocket quietly slipped a bullet home.

The orderly struggled with the muddy straps; at last, with a tug, the saddle came loose in his hands. And then, as young Tanner came forward, with an effort Broncho suddenly stood up.

Young Tanner paused, the destroyer in his hand. He gazed in mute astonishment at the horse, who stood trembling with exhaustion in front of him. And then, as he glanced into the suffering, lacklustre eye, something seemed to creep into it that he took to be the desire for life. And since, deep down, he was very human, he slipped that destroyer back into his pocket again.

'Well, I shan't pass sentence on you, at any rate,' he said under his breath.

Then he glanced round at his orderly.

'It seems to be a case for the hospital,' he said.

(From *Broncho*)

The Dealer's Yard

BY R. S. SURTEES

THE horses, as we said before, were almost all good flat-catchers, well calculated to please the eye, which Green knew was half the battle with the youngsters; and, moreover, like the aforesaid Bounding Ben, were generally christened with high-sounding names diametrically opposite to their respective qualities. Thus Everlasting, a handsome sixteen-hands horse, with black points, and all the shape and strength necessary for a weight-carrying hunter, slackened his pace as soon as ever he got upon rising ground, and gradually subsided into a walk as he ascended a hill. He couldn't go up one, so it was no use trying to force him.

Hearty Harry, again, wanted no end of coddling and linseed-teaing; Twice-a-week would hardly come out once a

94

fortnight; while The Glutton looked as if he had lived altogether upon toothpicks and water.

'That Boundin' Ben 'oss is most like big Mr R.'s work,' observed Peacock.

'Yes, he is,' assented Goodheart, 'yes, he is. Put him in as one.'

''Op Along, then,' suggested Aaron.

'Why, yes, he's a neat 'oss—a takin' 'oss—with a very high-bred determined hair about him,' replied Goodheart; 'but we mustn't call him 'Op Along, you know. Call him True Blue or Bell Metal or something of that sort.'

'Ah, Bell Metal's the better name—a very taking name. Bean him, and call him Bell Metal. He'll be No. 2. Now for another. Well, there's The Brick,' suggested Aaron.

'The Brick?' repeated Goodheart, for he had so many of that name that he could not hit off the horse at the moment.

'The brown 'oss with the star, and the dead side to his mouth—not the nutmeg grey that we bought off the soldier hofficer,' explained Peacock.

'Ah, that soldier officer's 'orse was a do,' sighed Goodheart; 'does nothin' but kick in the stable, and won't pass a wheeled vehicle of any sort or kind without scrubbin' his rider's leg up againt it, to see which is 'ardest. To be sure, he might do for a servant's 'oss,' continued he; 'servants aren't so 'tickler 'bout their legs as their masters; besides, there are no vehicles in the hunting-field for him to get to and scrub against. Oh, I would say christen him Perfection and send him,' said Goodheart.

'And The Brick?' asked Aaron.

'And The Brick too,' assented Goodheart. 'His only fault is that he won't face water, but a whip can always go round by a bridge, or across in a boat, or keep out of the way of water altogether. Then how about Oliver Twist?' continued Goodheart, pleased at the progress he was making.

'Oliver's not a bad 'oss,' replied Aaron, 'barrin' that his

forequarters are rather at wariance with his hind, but it don't make much matter which end of an 'oss gets through an 'edge fust, so long as they both land on the right side together at last.'

(From *Mr Facey Romford's Hounds*)

A Misdeal

BY E. O'E. SOMERVILLE AND MARTIN ROSS

'I BELIEVE I'm selling a horse here myself today,' said Flurry. 'Would you like to have a look at him, Mrs Yeates?'

'Oh, are you selling, Knox?' struck in Bernard, to whose brain the glory of buying a horse had mounted like new wine. 'I want another, and I know yours are the right sort.'

'Well, as you seem fond of galloping,' said Flurry sardonically, 'this one might suit you.'

'You don't mean the Moonlighter?' said Miss Knox, looking fixedly at him.

'Supposing I did, have you anything to say against him?' replied Flurry.

Decidedly he was in a very bad temper. Miss Sally shrugged her shoulders, and gave a little shred of a laugh, but said no more.

In a comparatively secluded corner of the field we came upon Moonlighter, sidling and fussing, with flickering ears, his tail tightly tucked in and his strong back humped in a manner that boded little good. Even to my untutored eye he appeared to be an uncommonly good-looking animal, a well-bred grey, with shoulders that raked back as far as the eye could wish, the true Irish jumping hindquarters, and a showy head and neck; it was obvious that nothing except Michael Hallahane's adroit chucks at his bridle kept him from displaying his jumping powers free of charge.

Bernard stared at him in silence; not the pregnant and intimidating silence of the connoisseur, but the tongue-tied muteness of helpless ignorance. His eye for horses had most probably been formed on circus posters, and the advertisments of a well-known embrocation, and Moonlighter approximated in colour and conduct to these models.

'I can see he's a ripping fine horse,' he said at length. 'I think I should like to try him.'

Miss Knox changed countenance perceptibly, and gave a perturbed glance at Flurry. Flurry remained impenetrably unamiable.

'I don't pretend to be a judge of horses,' went on Mr Shute. 'I dare say I needn't tell *you* that!' with a very engaging smile at Miss Sally; 'but I like this one awfully.'

As even Philippa said afterwards, she would not have given herself away like that over buying a reel of cotton.

'Are you quite sure that he's really the sort of horse you want?' said Miss Knox, with rather more colour in her face than usual. 'He's only four years old, and he's hardly a finished hunter.'

The object of her philanthropy looked rather puzzled. 'What! Can't he jump?' he said.

'Is it jump?' exclaimed Michael Hallahane, unable any longer to contain himself. 'Is it the horse that jumped five foot of a clothes-line in Hefferan's yard, and not a one on his back but himself, and didn't leave so much as the thrack of his hoof on the quilt that was hanging on it!'

'That's about good enough,' said Mr Shute with his large, friendly laugh. 'What's your price, Knox? I must have the horse that jumped the quilt! I'd like to try him, if you don't mind. There are some jolly-looking banks over there.'

'My price is a hundred sovereigns,' said Flurry; 'you can try him if you like.'

'Oh, don't!' cried Sally impulsively, but Bernard's foot was already in the stirrup. 'I call it disgraceful!' I heard her say in a low voice to her kinsman. 'You know he can't ride.'

The kinsman permitted himself a malign smile. 'That's his look out,' he said.

Perhaps the unexpected docility with which Moonlighter allowed himself to be manœuvred through the crowd was due to Bernard's thirteen stone; at all events, his progress through a gate into the next field was unexceptionable. Bernard, however, had no idea of encouraging this tranquility. He had come out to gallop, and without further ceremony he drove his heels into Moonlighter's side, and took the consequences in the shape of a very fine and able buck. How he remained within even visiting distance of the saddle it is impossible to explain; perhaps his early experience in the rigging stood him in good stead in the matter of hanging on by his hands; but, however preserved, he did remain, and went away down the field at what he himself subsequently described as 'the rate of knots'.

Flurry flung away his cigarette and ran to a point of better observation. We all ran, including Michael Hallahane and various onlookers, and were in time to see Mr Shute charging the least advantageous spot in a hollow-faced, furzy bank. Nothing but the grey horse's extreme activity got the pair safely over; he jumped it on a slant, changed feet in the heart of a furze-bush, and was lost to view. In what relative positions Bernard and his steed alighted was to us a matter of

conjecture. When we caught sight of them again, Moonlighter was running away, with his rider still on his back,
while the slope of the ground lent wings to his flight.

'That young gentleman will be apt to be killed,' said
Michael Hallahane with composure, not to say enjoyment.

'He'll be into the long bog with him pretty soon,' said
Flurry, his keen eye tracking the fugitive.

'Oh!—I thought he was off that time!' exclaimed Miss
Sally, with a gasp in which consternation and amusement
were blended. 'There! He *is* into the bog!'

It did not take us long to arrive at the scene of disaster, to
which, as to a dog-fight, other foot-runners were already
hurrying, and on our arrival we found things looking remarkably unpleasant for Mr Shute and Moonlighter. The
latter was sunk to his withers in the sheet of black slime into
which he had stampeded; the former, submerged to the
waist three yards farther away in the bog, was trying to drag
himself towards firm ground by the aid of tussocks of wiry
grass.

'Hit him!' shouted Flurry. 'Hit him! He'll sink if he stops
there!'

Mr Shute turned on his adviser a face streaming with black
mud, out of which his brown eyes and white teeth gleamed
with undaunted cheerfulness.

'All jolly fine!' he called back. 'If I let go this grass I'll
sink too!'

A shout of laughter from the male portion of the spectators
sympathetically greeted this announcement, and a dozen
equally futile methods of escape were suggested. Among
those who had joined us was, fortunately, one of the many
boys who pervaded the fair selling halters, and, by means of
several of these knotted together, a line of communication
was established. Moonlighter, who had fallen into the state
of inane stupor in which horses in his plight so often indulge,
was roused to activity by showers of stones and imprecations
but faintly chastened by the presence of ladies. Bernard,

hanging on to his tail, belaboured him with a cane, and, finally, the reins proving good, the task of towing the victims ashore was achieved.

'He's mine, Knox, you know,' were Mr Shute's first words as he scrambled to his feet; 'he's the best horse I ever got across—worth twice the money!'

'Faith, he's aisy plased!' remarked a bystander.

'Oh, do go and borrow some dry clothes,' interposed Philippa practically; 'surely there must be someone——'

'There's a shop in the town where he can strip a peg for thirteen and ninepence,' said Flurry grimly. 'I wouldn't care myself about the clothes you'd borrow here!'

The morning sun shone jovially upon Moonlighter and his rider, caking momentarily the black bog-stuff with which both were coated, and as the group disintegrated, and we turned to go back, every man present was pleasurably aware that the buttons of Mr Shute's riding-breeches had burst at the knee, causing a large triangular hiatus above his gaiter.

'Well,' said Flurry conclusively to me as we retraced our steps, 'I always thought the fellow was a fool, but I never thought he was such a damned fool.'

(From *Some Experiences of an Irish R.M.*)

Mr Soapey Sponge goes Horse-Coping
and acquires Ercles and Multum in Parvo

BY R. S. SURTEES

OUR readers will have the kindness to suppose our hero, Mr Sponge, shot out of an omnibus at the sign of the Cat and Compasses, in the full rurality of grass country, sprinkled with fallows and turnip fields. We should state that this unwonted journey was a desire to pay a visit to Mr Benjamin Buckram, the horse-dealer's farm at Scampley, distant some mile and a half from where he was set down, a space that he now purposed travelling on foot.

Mr Benjamin Buckram was a small horse-dealer—small, at least, when he was buying, though great when he was selling. It would do a youngster good to see Ben filling the two capacities. He dealt in second-hand, that is to say, past mark of mouth horses; but on the present occasion Mr Sponge sought his services in the capacity of a letter rather than a seller of horses. Mr Sponge wanted to job a couple of plausible-looking horses, with the option of buying them, provided he (Mr Sponge) could sell them for more than he would have to give Mr Buckram, exclusive of hire. Mr Buckram's job price, we should say, was as near twelve pounds a month, containing twenty-eight days, as he could screw, the hirer, of course, keeping the animals.

Scampley is one of those pretty little suburban farms, peculiar to the north and north-west side of London—farms varying from fifty to a hundred acres of well-manured, gravelly soil; each farm with its picturesque little buildings, consisting of small, honeysuckled, rose-entwined brick houses with small, flat, pantiled roofs and lattice-windows; and, hard by, a large haystack, three times the size of the house, or a desolate barn, half as big as all the rest of the buildings. From the smallness of the holdings, the farmhouses are dotted about as thickly, and at such varying distances from the roads, as to look like inferior 'villas' falling out of rank; most of them have a half-smart, half-seedy sort of look.

The rustics who cultivate them, or rather look after them, are neither exactly town nor country. They have the clownish dress and boorish gait of the regular 'chaws', with a good deal of the quick, suspicious, sour sauciness of the low London resident. If you can get an answer from them at all, it is generally delivered in such a way as to show that the answerer thinks you are what they call 'chaffing' them, asking them what you know.

These farms serve the double purpose of purveyors to the London stables, and hospitals for sick, overworked or unsaleable horses. All the great job-masters and horse-dealers have these retreats in the country, and the smaller ones pretend to have, from whence, in due course, they can draw any sort of an animal a customer may want, just as little cellarless wine-merchants can get you any sort of wine from the real establishments—if you only give them time.

There was a good deal of mystery about Scampley. It was sometimes in the hands of Mr Benjamin Buckram, sometimes in the hands of his assignees, sometimes in those of his cousin Abraham Brown, and sometimes John Doe and Richard Roe were the occupants of it.

Mr Benjamin Buckram, though very far from being one, had the advantage of looking like a respectable man. There was a certain plump, well-fed rosiness about him which, aided by a bright-coloured dress, joined to a continual fumble in the pockets of his drab trousers, gave him the air of a 'well-to-do-in-the-world' sort of man. Moreover, he sported a velvet collar to his blue coat, a more imposing ornament than it appears at first sight. To be sure, there are two sorts of velvet collars—the legitimate velvet collar, commencing with the coat, and the adopted velvet collar, put on when the cloth one gets shabby.

Buckram's was always the legitimate velvet collar, new from the first; and, we really believe, a permanent velvet collar, adhered to in storm and in sunshine, has a very money-making impression upon the world. It shows a spirit superior to feelings of paltry economy, and we think a person would be much more excusable for being victimized by a man with a good velvet collar to his coat, than by one exhibiting that spurious sign of gentility—a horse and gig.

The reader will now have the kindness to imagine Mr Sponge arriving at Scampley.

'Ah, Mr Sponge!' exclaimed Mr Buckram, who, having seen our friend advancing up the little twisting approach from the road to his house through a little square window almost blinded with Irish ivy, out of which he was in the habit of contemplating the arrival of his occasional lodgers, Doe and Roe, 'Ah, Mr Sponge!' exclaimed he, with well-assumed gaiety, 'you should have been here yesterday; sent away two sich 'osses—perfect 'unters—the werry best

I do think I ever saw in my life; either would have bin the
werry 'oss for your money. But come in, Mr Sponge, sir,
come in,' continued he, backing himself through a little
sentry-box of a green portico, to a narrow passage which
branched off into little rooms on either side.

As Buckram made this retrograde movement he gave a
gentle pull to the wooden handle of an old-fashioned wire
bell-pull, in the midst of buggy, four-in-hand and other
whips, hanging in the entrance; a touch that was acknowledged by a single tinkle of the bell in the stable yard.

They then entered the little room on the right, whose walls
were decorated with various sporting prints, chiefly illustra-
tive of steeplechases, with here and there a stunted fox-brush,
tossing about as a duster. The ill-ventilated room reeked
with the effluvia of stale smoke, and the faded green baize
of a little round table in the centre was covered with filbert-
shells and empty ale glasses. The whole furniture of the room
wasn't worth five pounds.

Mr Sponge, being now on the dealing tack, commenced in
the poverty-stricken strain adapted to the occasion. Having
deposited his hat on the floor, taken up his leg to nurse and
given his hair a backward rub with his right hand, he thus
commenced:

'Now, Buckram,' said he, 'I'll tell you how it is. I'm
deuced hard up—regularly in Short's Gardens. I lost
eighteen 'undred on the Derby, and seven on the Leger, the
best part of my year's income, indeed; and I just want to
hire two or three horses for the season, with the option of
buying, if I like; and if you supply me well, I may be the
means of bringing grist to your mill; you twig, eh?'

'Well, Mr Sponge,' replied Buckram, sliding several con-
secutive half-crown down the incline plane of his pocket.
'Well, Mr Sponge, I shall be happy to do my best for you. I
wish you'd come yesterday, though, as I said before. I jest
had two of the neatest nags—a bay and a grey—not that
colour makes any matter to a judge like you; there's no

sounder saying than that a good 'oss is not never of a bad colour; only to a young gemman, you know, it's well to have 'em smart, and the ticket, in short; howsomever, I must do the best I can for you, and if there's nothin' in that tickles your fancy, why, you must give me a few days to see if I can arrange an exchange with some other gent; but the present is like to be a werry haggiwatin' season; had more happlications for 'osses nor ever I remembers, and I've been a dealer now, man and boy, turned of eight-and-thirty years; but young gents is whimsical, and it was a young'un wot got these, and there's no sayin' but he mayn't like them—indeed, one's rayther difficult to ride—that's to say, the grey, the neatest of the two, and he *may* come back, and if so, you shall have him; and a safer, sweeter 'oss was never seen, or one more like to do credit to a gent; but you knows what an 'oss is, Mr Sponge, and can do justice to one, and *I* should like to put summut good into your hands—*that* I should.'

With conversation, or rather with balderdash, such as this, Mr Buckram beguiled the few minutes necessary for removing the bandages, hiding the bottles, and stirring up the cripples about to be examined, and the heavy flap of the coach-house door announcing that all was ready, he forthwith led the way through a door in a brick wall into a little three-sides of a square yard, formed of stables and loose-boxes, with a delapidated dove-cote above a pump in the centre; Mr Buckram, not growing corn, could afford to keep pigeons.

ii

Nothing bespeaks the character of a dealer's trade more than the servants and hangers-on of the establishment. The civiler in manner, and the better they are 'put on', the higher the standing of the master, and the better the stamp of the horses.

Those about Mr Buckram's were of a very shady order.

Dirty-shirted, sloggering, baggy-breeched, slangey-gaitered fellows, with the word 'gin' indelibly printed on their faces. Peter Leather, the head man, was one of the fallen angels of servitude. He had once driven a duke—the Duke of Dazzleton —having nothing whatsoever to do but dress himself and climb into his well-indented richly-fringed throne, with a helper at each horse's head to 'let go' at a nod from his broad-laced three-cornered hat. Then, having got in his cargo (or rubbish, as he used to call them), he would start off at a pace that was truly terrific, cutting out this vehicle, shooting past that, all but grazing a third, anathematizing the buses and abusing the draymen. We don't know how he might be with the Queen, but he certainly drove as though he thought nobody had any business in the street while the Duchess of Dazzleton wanted it. The Duchess liked going fast, and Peter accommodated her. The duke jobbed his horses and didn't care about pace, and so things might have gone on very comfortably, if Peter one afternoon hadn't run his pole into the panel of a very plain but very neat yellow barouche, passing the end of New Bond Street, which having nothing but a simple crest—a stag's head on the panel—made him think it belonged to some bulky cit, taking the air with his rib; but who, unfortunately, turned out to be no less a person than Sir Giles Nabem, Knight, the great police magistrate: upon one of whose myrmidons in plain clothes, who came to the rescue, Peter committed a most violent assault—for which unlucky casualty his worship furnished him with rotatory occupation for his fat calves in the 'H. of C.', as the clerk shortly designated the House of Correction.

Thither Peter went, and in lieu of his lace-bedaubed coat, gold-gartered plushes, stockings and buckled shoes, he was dressed up in a suit of tight-fitting yellow and black striped worsteds, that gave him the appearance of a wasp without wings.

Peter Leather then tumbled regularly down the staircase of

servitude, the greatness of his fall being occasionally broken
by landing in some inferior place. From the Duke of Dazzleton's, or rather from the treadmill, he went to the Marquis of
Mammon, whom he very soon left because he wouldn't wear
a second-hand wig. From the marquis he got hired to the
great Irish Earl of Coarsegab, who expected him to wash the
carriage, wait at table and do other incidentals never contemplated by a London coachman. Peter threw this place up
with indignation on being told to take the letters to the post.
He then lived on his 'means', a thing that is much finer in
theory than in practice, and having about exhausted his
substance and placed the bulk of his apparel in safe keeping,
he condescended to take a place as job coachman in a
livery stable—a 'horses let by the hour, day or month' one,
in which he enacted as many characters, at least made as
many different appearances, as the late Mr Matthews used
to do in his celebrated 'At Homes'. One day Peter would be
seen ducking under the mews entrance in one of those
greasy, painfully well-brushed hats, the certain precursors
of soiled linen and seedy, most seedy-covered, buttoned
coats, that would puzzle a conjurer to say whether they were
black, or grey, or olive, or invisible green turned visible
brown. Then another day he might be seen in old Mrs
Gadabout's sky-blue livery, with a tarnished, gold-laced hat
nodding over his nose; and on the third he would shine
forth in Mrs Major-General Flareup's cockaded one, with a
worsted shoulder-knot, and a much over-daubed light drab
livery coat with crimson inexpressibles, so tight as to astonish
a beholder how he ever got into them.

Humiliation, however, has its limits as well as other
things, and Peter, having been invited to descend from his
box—alas! a regular country patent-leather one—and invest
himself in a Quaker-collared blue coat, with a red vest and a
pair of blue trousers with a broad red stripe down the sides,
to drive the Honourable old Miss Wrinkleton, of Harley
Street, to Court in a 'one-'oss pianoforte-case' as he called a

Clarence, could stand it no longer; and, chucking the nether garments into the fire, he rushed frantically up the area steps, mounted his box, and quilted the old crocodile of a horse all the way home, accompanying each cut with an imprecation such as '*Me* make a guy of myself!' (whip) '*Me* put on sich things!' (whip, whip) '*Me* drive down Sin Jimses Street!' (whip, whip, whip), '*I'd* see her —— fust!' (whip, whip, whip), cutting at the old horse just as if he was laying it into Miss Wrinkleton, so that by the time he got home he had established a considerable lather on the old nag, which, his master resenting, a row ensued, the sequel of which may readily be imagined. After assisting Mrs Clearstarch, the Kilburn laundress, in getting in and taking out her washing for a few weeks, chance at last landed him at Mr Benjamin Buckram's, from whence he is now about to be removed to become our hero Mr Sponge's Sancho Panza, in his fox-hunting, fortune-hunting career, and disseminate in remote parts his doctrines of the real honour and dignity of servitude. Now to the inspection.

Peter Leather, having a peep-hole as well as his master, on seeing Mr Sponge arrive had given himself an extra rub over, and covered his dirty shirt with a clean, well-tied white kerchief, and a whole coloured scarlet waistcoat, late the property of one of his noble employers, in hopes that Sponge's visit might lead to something. Peter was about sick of the suburbs, and thought, of course, that he couldn't be worse off than where he was.

'Here's Mr Sponge wants some 'osses,' observed Mr Buckram, as Leather met them in the middle of the little yard and brought his right arm round with a sort of military swing to his forehead. 'What 'ave we in?' continued Buckram, with the air of a man with so many horses that he didn't know what were in and what were out.

'Vy we 'ave Rumbleton in,' replied Leather thoughtfully, stroking down his hair as he spoke, 'and we 'ave Jack o'Lantern in, and we 'ave the Camel in, and there's the

little Hirish 'oss with the sprig tail—Jack-a-Dandy, as I calls
him—and the Flyer will be in tonight, he's jest out a hairing,
as it were, with old Mr Callipash.'

'Ah, Rumbleton won't do for Mr Sponge,' observed
Buckram thoughtfully, at the same time letting go a tremendous avalanche of silver down his trouser pocket.
'Rumbleton won't do,' repeated he, 'nor Jack-a-Dandy
nouther.'

'Why, I wouldn't commend neither on 'em,' replied
Peter, taking his cue from his master, 'only ven you axes me
vot there's in, you knows vy I must give you a *cor*-rect
answer, in course.'

'In course,' nodded Buckram.

Leather and Buckram had a good understanding in the
lying line, and had fallen into a sort of tacit arrangement,
that if the former was staunch about the horses he was at
liberty to make the best terms he could for himself. Whatever
Buckram said, Leather swore to, and they had established
certain signals and expressions that each understood.

'I've an unkimmon nice 'oss,' at length observed Mr
Buckram, with a scrutinizing glance at Sponge, 'and an 'oss
in hevery respect werry like your work, but he's an 'oss I'll
candidly state, I wouldn't put in everyone's 'ands; for, in the
fust place, he's wery walueous, and in the second, he requires
an 'ossman to ride; howsomever, as I knows that you *can*
ride, and if you doesn't mind taking my ead man'—
jerking his elbow at Leather—'to look arter him, I wouldn't
mind 'commodatin' on you, *provided* we can 'gree upon
terms.'

'Well, let's see him,' interrupted Sponge, 'and we can
talk about terms after.'

'Certainly, sir, certainly,' replied Buckram, again letting
loose a re-accumulated rush of silver down his pocket.
'Here, Tom! Joe! Harry! where's Sam?' giving the little
tinkler of a bell a pull as he spoke.

'Sam be in the straw-'ouse,' replied Leather, passing

through a stable into a wooden projection beyond, where the gentleman in question was enjoying a nap.

'Sam!' said he, '*Sam!*' repeated he, in a louder tone, as he saw the object of his search's nose popping through the midst of the straw.

'*What now!*' exclaimed Sam, starting up and looking wildly round. 'What now?' repeated he, rubbing his eyes with the backs of his hands.

'Get our Ercles,' said Leather, *sotto voce*.

The lad was a mere stripling—some fifteen or sixteen years, perhaps—tall, slight and neat, with dark hair and eyes, and was dressed in a brown jacket—a real boy's jacket, without laps, white cords and top-boots. It was his business to risk his neck and limbs at all hours of the day, on all sorts of horses, over any sort of place that any person chose to require him to put a horse at, and this he did with the daring pleasure of youth as yet undaunted by any serious fall. Sam now bestirred himself to get out the horse. The clambering of hoofs presently announced his approach.

Whether Hercules was called Hercules on account of his amazing strength, or from a fanciful relationship to the famous horse of that name, we know not; but his strength and his colour would favour either supposition. He was an immense, tall, powerful, dark brown, sixteen-hands horse, with an arched neck and crest, well set on, clean, lean head, and loins that looked as if they could shoot a man into the next country. His condition was perfect. His coat lay as close and even as satin, with cleanly-developed muscle, and altogether he looked as hard as a cricket-ball. He had a famous switch tail, reaching nearly to his hocks, and making him look less than he would otherwise have done.

Mr Sponge was too well-versed in horse-flesh to imagine that such an animal would be in the possession of such a third-rate dealer as Buckram, unless there was something radically wrong about him, and as Sam and Leather were paying the horse those stable attentions that always precede a show-out, Mr Sponge settled in his own mind that the observation about his requiring a horseman to ride him meant that he was vicious. Nor was he wrong in his anticipations, for not all Leather's whistlings, or Sam's endearings and watchings, could conceal the sunken, scowling eye, that as good as said, 'You'd better keep clear of me.'

Mr Sponge, however, was a dauntless horseman. What man dared he dared, and as the horse stepped proudly and freely out of the stable, Mr Sponge thought he looked very like a hunter. Nor were Mr Buckram's laudations wanting in the animal's behalf.

'There's an 'orse!' exclaimed he, drawing his right hand out of his trouser pocket and flourishing it towards him. 'If that 'orse were down in Leicestersheer,' added he, 'he'd fetch three 'under'd guineas. Sir Richard would have him in a minnit—*that he would!*' added he, with a stamp of his foot as he saw the animal beginning to set up his back and wince at the approach of the lad. (We may here mention, by way of parenthesis, that Mr Buckram had bought him out of Warwicksheer for thirty pounds, where the horse had greatly distinguished himself, as well by kicking off sundry scarlet swells in the gaily-thronged streets of Leamington, as by running away with divers others over the wide-stretching grazing-grounds of Southam and Dunchurch.)

But to our story. The horse now stood staring on view: fire in his eye, and vigour in his every limb. Leather at his head, the lad at his side, Sponge and Buckram a little on the left.

'*W-h-o-a-a-y*, my man, *w-h-o-a-a-y,*' continued Mr Buckram, as a liberal show of the white of the eye was followed by a little wince and hoist of the hindquarters on the nearer approach of the lad.

'*Look sharp, boy,*' said he, in a very different tone to the soothing one in which he had just been addressing the horse. The lad lifted up his leg for a hoist, Leather gave him one as quick as thought, and led on the horse as the lad gathered up his reins. They then made for a large field at the back of the house, with leaping-bars, hurdles, 'on and offs', 'in and outs', all sorts of fancy leaps scattered about. Having got him fairly in, and the lad having got himself fairly settled in the saddle, he gave the horse a touch with the spur as Leather let go his head, and after a desperate plunge or two started off at a gallop.

'*He's fresh,*' observed Mr Buckram confidentially to Mr Sponge, 'he's fresh—wants work, in short—short of work—wouldn't put everyone on him—wouldn't put one o' your timid Cocknified chaps on him, for if ever he were to get the hupper 'and, vy I doesn't know as ow that we might get the hupper 'and o' him, agen, but the playful rogue knows ven he's got a workman on his back—see how he gives to the lad though he's only fifteen, and not strong of his hage nouther,' continued Mr Buckram, 'and I guess if he had sich a con-sternation of talent as you on his back, he'd wery soon be as quiet as a lamb—not that he's wicious—far from it, only play—full of play, I may say, though to be sure, if a man gets spilt it don't argufy much whether it's done from play or from wice.'

Having gone through the usual routine, the lad now walked the glowing-coated, snorting horse back to where the trio stood. Mr Sponge again looked him over, and still seeing no exception to take to him, bid the lad get off, and lengthen the stirrups for him to take a ride. That was the difficulty. The first two minutes always did it. Mr Sponge, however, nothing daunted, borrowed Sam's spurs, and made Leather hold the horse by the head till he got well into the saddle, and then lead him on a bit; he gave the animal such a dig in both sides as fairly threw him off his guard, and made him start away at a gallop, instead of standing and delivering, as was his wont.

Away Mr Sponge shot, pulling him about, trying all his paces, and putting him at all sorts of leaps.

Emboldened by the nerve and dexterity displayed by Mr

Sponge, Mr Buckram stood meditating a further trial of his equestrian ability, as he watched him bucketing Ercles about. Hercules had 'spang-hewed' so many triers, and the hideous contraction of his resolute back had deterred so many from mounting, that Buckram had begun to fear he would have to place him in the only remaining school for incurables, the 'bus. Hack-horse riders are seldom great horsemen. The very fact of their being hack-horse riders shows they are little accustomed to horses, or they would not give the fee-simple of an animal for a few weeks' work.

'I've a wonderful clever little 'oss,' observed Mr Buckram, as Sponge returned with a slack rein and a satisfied air on the late resolute animal's back. '*Little* I can 'ardly call 'im,' continued Mr Buckram, 'only he's low; but you knows that the 'eight of an 'oss has nothin' to do with his size. Now this is a perfect dray-'oss in miniature. An 'Arrow gent, lookin' at him, t'other day christen'd him Multum in Parvo. But though he's so *ter-men-dous* strong, he has the knack o' going, specially in deep; and if you're not a-goin' to Sir Richard, but into some o'them plough sheers (shires), I'd 'commend him to you.'

'Let's have a look at him,' replied Mr Sponge, throwing his right leg over Hercules' head, and sliding from the saddle on to the ground, as if he were alighting from the quietest shooting-pony in the world.

All then was hurry, scurry and scamper to get this second prodigy out. Presently he appeared. Multum in Parvo was certainly all that Buckram described him. A long, low, clean-headed, clean-necked, big-hocked chestnut, with a long tail and great, large, flat, white legs, without mark or blemish upon them. Unlike Hercules, there was nothing indicative of vice or mischief about him. Indeed, he was rather a sedate, meditative-looking animal; and, instead of the watchful, arm's-length sort of way Leather and Co. treated Hercules, they jerked and pulled Parvo about as if he were a cow.

Still Parvo had his foibles. He was a resolute, head-strong animal, that would go his own way in spite of all the pulling and hauling in the world. If he took it into his obstinate head to turn into a particular field, into it he would be; or against the gate-post he would bump the rider's leg in a way that would make him remember the difference of opinion between them. His was not a fiery, hot-headed spirit, with object or reason for its guide, but just a regular downright pig-headed sort of stupidity that nobody could account for. He had a mouth like a bull, and would walk clean through a gate sometimes rather than be at the trouble of rising to leap it; at other times he would hop over it like a bird. He could not beat Mr Buckram's men, because they were always on the look-out for objects of contention with sharp spur rowels, ready to let into his sides the moment he began to stop; but a weak or a timid man on his back had no more chance than he would on an elephant. If the horse chose to carry him into the midst of hounds at the meet, he would have him in—nay, he would think nothing of upsetting the master himself in the middle of the pack. Then the provoking part was that the obstinate animal, after having done all the mischief, would just set-to to eat as if nothing had happened. After rolling a sportsman in the mud he would repair to the nearest haystack or grassy bank, and be caught. He was now ten years old, or a *leetle* more perhaps, and very wicked years some of them had been. His adventures, his sellings and his returnings, his lettings and his unletting, his bumpings and spillings, his smashings and crashings, on the road, in the field, in single and double harness, would furnish a volume of themselves; and in default of a more able historian, we purpose blending his future fortune with that of Ercles, in the service of our hero Mr Sponge, and his accomplished groom, and undertaking the important narration of them ourselves.

(From *Mr Sponge's Sporting Tour*)

'Your Handwriting, Sir'

BY G. J. WHYTE-MELVILLE

'Morning, sir,' says Mr Sloper, scenting a customer as he accosts his guest. 'Oh, it's you, is it, Mr Sawyer? Won't ye step in and set down after your walk? Take a glass of mild ale and a crust of bread and cheese, or a drop of sherry or anythink?'

'No hunting today, Job,' answers the visitor, declining the refreshment, 'so I just toddled over to see how you're getting on, and have a look round the stables; no harm in looking, you know.'

Mr Sloper's face assumes an expression of profound mystery. 'I'm glad you come over today, sir,' he says, in a tone of confidential frankness, 'of all days in the year. I've a 'orse here, as I should like to ast your opinion about—a gent like *you* as knows what a 'unter really is. And so you should, Mr

Sawyer, for there's no man alive takes greater liberties with 'em when they *can* go and do it. And I've got one in that box, as *I* think, just *is* more than curious.'

'Would he carry *me*?' asks Mr Sawyer, with well-affected indifference, as if he had not come over expressly to find one that would. 'Not that I *want* a horse, you know; but if I saw one I liked very much, and you didn't price him too high, why I *might* be induced to buy against next season, perhaps.'

Job took his hands out of his coat pockets, and spread them abroad, as it were to dry. The action denoted extreme purity and candour.

'No; I don't think as he ought to carry *you*, sir,' was the unexpected reply. 'Now, I ain't a-going to tell you a lie, Mr Sawyer. This horse didn't *ought* to be ridden, not the way *you* take and ride them, Mr Sawyer; leastways not over such a blind heart-breaking country as this here. He's too good, he is, for that kind of work; he ought to be in Leicestershire, *he* ought; the Harborough country, that's the country for him. He's too fast for *us*, and that's the truth. Only, to be sure, we have a vast of plough hereabout, and *I* never see such a sticker through dirt. It makes no odds to him, pasture *or* plough, and the sweetest hack I ever clapped eyes on besides. However, you shall judge for yourself, Mr Sawyer. I won't ask you to believe *me*. You've a quicker eye to a horse than I have, by a long chalk, and I'd sooner have your opinion than my own. I *would* now, and that's the truth!'

Our purchaser began to think that he might possibly have hit upon *the* animal at last. Often as he had been at the game, and often as he had been disappointed, he was still sanguine enough to believe he might draw the prize-ticket in the lottery at any time. As I imagine every man who pulls on his boots to go out hunting has a sort of vague hope that today may be his day of triumph with the hounds, so the oldest and wariest of us cannot go into a dealer's yard without a sort of half-conscious idea that there *must* be a trump card somewhere in the pack, and it *may* be our luck to hold it as well as another's.

But Sloper, like the rest of his trade, was not going to show his game first. It seems to be a maxim with all salesmen to prove their customers with inferior articles before they come to the real thing. Mr Sawyer had to walk through a four-stall stable, and inspect, preparatory to declining, a mealy bay cob, a lame grey, a broken-winded chestnut, and an enormous brown animal, very tall, very narrow, very ugly, with extremely upright forelegs and shoulders to match. The latter his owner affirmed to be '*an extraordinary shaped 'un*', as no doubt he was. A little playful badinage on the merits of this last enlivened the visit.

'What will you take for the brown, Sloper, if I buy him at so much a foot?' said the customer, as they emerged into the fresh air.

'Say ten pound a foot, sir!' answered Job, with the utmost gravity, 'and ten over, because *he always has a foot to spare*. Come now, Mr Sawyer, I can afford to let a good customer like you have that horse for *fefty*. *Fefty* guineas, or even *pounds*, sir, to *you*. I got him in a bad debt, you see, sir—it's Bible truth I'm telling ye—and he only stood *me* in forty-seven pounds ten, *and* a sov. I gave the man as brought him over. He's not everybody's horse, Mr Sawyer, that isn't; but I think he'll carry *you* remarkably well.'

'I don't think I'll ever give him the chance,' was the rejoinder. 'Come, Job, we're burning daylight; let's go and have a look at the crack.'

One individual had been listening to the above conversation with thrilling interest. This was no less a personage than Barney, Mr Sloper's head groom, general factotum and rough-rider in ordinary—an official whose business it was to ride anything *at* anything, for anybody who asked him. He was a little old man, with one eye, a red handkerchief, and the general appearance of a post-boy on half pay; a sober fellow too, and as brave as King Richard; yet had he expressed himself strongly about this said brown horse, the previous evening, to the maid-of-all-work. 'It's nateral for 'em to fall; but when *he* falls, he's all over a chap till he's crumpled him.' So his heroic heart beat more freely when they adjourned to the neighbouring box.

Mr Sloper threw the door open with an air. It must be confessed he seldom had one that would bear, without preparation, a minute inspection from the eye of a sportsman; but he knew *this* was a sound one, and made the most of it. Clothed and hooded, littered to the hocks, and sheeted to the tail, there was yet something about his general appearance that fascinated Mr Sawyer at once. Job saw the spell was working, and abstained from disturbing it. As far as could be seen, the animal was a long, low, well-bred-looking roan, with short, flat legs, large, clean hocks, and swelling muscular thighs. His supple skin threw off a bloom, as if he was in first-rate condition; and when, laying his ears back and biting the manger, he lifted a foreleg, as it were, to expostulate with his visitors, the hoof was round, open, and well developed, as blue, and to all appearance as hard, as a flint.

'Has he *fashion* enough, think you, sir?' asked Job at length, breaking the silence. 'Strip him, Barney,' he added, taking the straw from his mouth.

The roan winced and stamped, and whisked his tail, and set his back up during the process; but when it was concluded, Mr Sawyer could not but confess to himself, that if he was only as good as he *looked*, he would *do*.

'Feel his legs, Mr Sawyer!' observed the dealer, turning away to conceal the triumph that *would* ooze out. 'There's some legs—there's some hocks and thighs! Talk of loins, and look where his tail's set on. Carries his *own* head, too; and *if* you could see his manners! I never saw such manners in the hunting-field. Six-year-old—not a speck or blemish; bold as a bull, and gentle as a lady; he can go as fast as you can clap your hands, and stay till the middle of the week after next—jump a town, too, and never turn his head from the place you put him at. As handy as a fiddle, as neat as a pink, and worth all the money to carry in your eye when you go out to buy hunters. But what's the use of talking about it to a judge like you? Lay your leg over him—only just lay your leg over him, Mr Sawyer. I don't want you to buy him! but get on him and feel his action, just as a favour to *me*.'

Our friend had made up his mind he would do so from the first. There was no mistaking the appearance of the animal; so good was it, that he had but two misgivings—some rank unsoundness, to account for its being there, or so high a price as to be beyond his means; for Mr Sawyer was too fond of the sport to give a sum that he could not replace for so perishable an article as a hunter.

He was no mean equestrian, our friend, and quite at home on a strange horse. As he drew the curb-rein gently through his fingers, the roan dropped his long, lean head, and champed the bit playfully, tossing a speck of froth back on his rider's boots.

'You've got a mouth, at any rate,' quoth Mr Sawyer, and trotted him gently down the hard road, the animal stepping freely and gaily under him, full of life and spirits. The customer liked his mount, and couldn't help showing it. 'May I lark him?' said he, pulling up after a short canter to and fro on the turf by the wayside; during which Job Sloper had been exercising his mental arithmetic in what we may term a sum of problematical addition.

'Take him into the close, sir,' was the generous reply; 'put him at anything you like. If you can get him into one of those fences, I'll *give* him to you!'

So Mr Sawyer sat down to jump a low hedge and ditch, then stood him, and caught hold of the roan's head, and sent him a cracker through the adjoining plough, and across a larger fence into a pasture, and back again over a fair flight of rails and lost his flat shooting-hat, and rucked his plaid trousers up to his knees; and Sloper marked his kindling eye and glowing cheek, and knew that he had *landed* him.

'Walk him about for ten minutes before you do him over,' said that worthy to Barney, as Mr Sawyer dismounted, and the latter brought him his hat. 'And now sir,' added the hospitable dealer, 'you can't go away without tasting my cheese—the same you liked last time, you know. Walk in, sir; this way, and mind the step, if *you* please.' So speaking, Mr Sloper led the way into a neat little parlour with a strong odour of preserved tobacco smoke, where a clean cloth set off a nice luncheon of bread and cheese, flanked by a foaming jug of strong ale and a decanter of oily-brown sherry.

And herein the dealer showed his knowledge of human nature, and his discrimination in the different character-istics of the species. Had his guest been some generous scion of the aristocracy, with more money than nerves, he would have *primed* him first, and put him up to ride afterwards. But he knew his man. He was well aware that Mr Sawyer required no stimulant to make him jump, but a strong one to induce him to part with his money; so he proposed the luncheon after he was satisfied that his customer was pleased with his mount.

Neither of them touched on business during the meal, the conversation consisting chiefly of the runs that had lately taken place in the old country, with many as inferred com-pliment to the good riding of the possible purchaser. Then Mr Sawyer produced the Larranagas and offered one to Job, who bit it, and wet it, and smoked it, as men do who are more used to clay pipes, and then they went back to the stable to see the roan done up.

The gallop and the ale were working in Mr Sawyer's brain, but he didn't see his way into the roan at a hundred; so he obstinately held his tongue. The dealer was obliged to break the ice.

'I'd take it very friendly of you, sir, if you'd give me your honest opinion of that horse,' said he, waving the Larranaga towards the animal. 'I fancy he's too good for our country; and I've a brother-in-law down in Rutland as wants to have him very bad. He's just the cut, so he says, for these Melton gents; and he's a good judge, is my brother-in-law, and a pretty rider to boot. He'd give me my price, too; but then, you know, sir, askin' your pardon, it isn't always ready money between relations; and that cuts the other way again, as a man may say. What do *you* think, Mr Sawyer?'

'I'll find out what he wants for him, at any rate,' thought the customer. 'What's his figure?' was the abrupt rejoinder.

Mr. Sloper hesitated. 'A hundred and'—*eighty*, he was going to say; but seeing his customer's eye resting on the roan's back-ribs—a point in which the horse was somewhat deficient—he dropped at once to seventy, and regretted it the next moment when he caught the expression of the listener's face.

'It isn't *even* money,' answered Mr Sawyer, without, however, making the same sort of face he had done several times before, when he had refused to give double the sum at which he eventually purchased. 'I should say you might get a hundred and twenty for him down there, if you'd luck. But it's a great risk—a great risk—and a long distance; and perhaps have him sent back to you in the spring. If I wanted a horse, *I'd* give you a hundred for him, though he isn't exactly my sort. A hundred!—I'll tell you what, Sloper, I'll be hanged if I won't *chance* it—I'll *give* you a hundred—*guineas*—come! Money down, and no questions asked.'

'I can warrant him sound,' answered Mr Sloper, 'and I'd rather *you* had him than anybody. But it's childish talking of a hundred guineas and that horse on the same afternoon. However, I thank you kindly all the same, Mr Sawyer. Barney! shut the box up. Come in, sir, and have *one* glass of sherry before you start. The evenings get chill at this time of the year, and that's old sherry, and won't hurt you no more than milk. He *is* a nice horse, Mr Sawyer, I think— a *very* nice horse, and I'm glad you're pleased with him.'

So they returned into the little parlour, and stirred up the fire, and finished the bottle of old sherry: nor is it necessary to remark that, with the concluding glass of that generous fluid the roan became the property of John Standish Sawyer, under the following somewhat complicated agreement: That he was to give an immediate cheque for a hundred and forty pounds, and ten pounds more at the end of the season; which later donation was to be increased to twenty if he should sell him for anything over two hundred—a contingency which the dealer was pleased to observe amounted to what he called 'a moral'.

The new owner went to look at him once more in the stable, and thought him the nicest horse he ever saw in his life. The walk home, too, was delightful, till the sherry had evaporated, when it became rather tedious; and at dinnertime Mr Sawyer was naturally less hungry than thirsty. All the evening, however, he congratulated himself on having done a good day's work. All night, too, he dreamed of the roan; and on waking resolved to call him Hotspur.

When the horse came home next day, he certainly looked rather smaller than his new owner had fancied. Old Isaac, too, growled out his untoward opinion that he 'looked a sort as would work very *light*'. But then Isaac always grumbled —it was the old groom's way of enjoying himself.

(From *Market Harborough*)

Cahirmee Fair

BY 'SPIDER' JACOBSON

I WONDER how many people outside 'the trade', or horse dealers, have actually witnessed a fair in Ireland. For anyone who is at all interested in the study of human nature it's the most amusing way of spending a few days. Some years ago I went to Cahirmee Fair; why it's called Cahirmee when it's held in Buttevant I can't tell you; there are many things to do with Ireland and the Irish which are quite inexplicable, but withal it's a delightful country and I love the Irish.

I went over on this particular occasion with a dealer called Palmer. We eventually arrived at Mallow, which is on the main line, and we took a car out to Buttevant. Before all the disturbances in Ireland Buttevant was an extremely prosperous little place as it was a military depot, having quite a large barracks at the top end of the village. These, needless to say, during the days of the Sinn Feiners were burnt down to the ground, and as far as I know have not been touched since then. When I saw the place last the inhabitants were all broke and there wasn't one who didn't bewail the good old days when 'the military were in it'. Now, I fancy, they live a more or less hand-to-mouth existence, but with all their vicissitudes they succeed in remaining extremely cheerful.

Next door to the ruins of the barracks is the hotel. Now I haven't a very vast experience of hotels in small places in Ireland, but I can well imagine that if they are on a par with this one that touring in Ireland might not be too comfortable a business. We were greeted by what I took to be the waitress. I found out afterwards that she was, among other things. She waited, fetched the food, did the beds, got you hot water to shave in—that's to say, you got it 'if she could but dodge the cook, who was a terrible woman these times'. She also assisted in the office in her spare moments. Never once during the three days I was there did I see her anything but aimiable, and I very much doubt if she ever went to bed at all. If you were up early she was up before you, if you returned very late she was still there serving food and drinks.

You cannot exactly call the hotel a palace. It has just one general room where one eats, smokes, talks or writes letters. Upstairs are the bedrooms and, the pride of the place, the bathroom. I had a look at it and could not quite make up my mind off-hand whether it would be cleaner to have a bath or not; and I left the matter to decide itself on the following morning.

Palmer and I had some food, and once more I wondered why it was that a potato boiled by an Irish cook in Ireland tastes entirely different to a potato cooked by anyone in any other part of the world. Now I frankly admit I'm greedy. I don't go so far as to say I make a hog of myself—still, since to live you must eat, it has always seemed to me to be common sense that you should eat as well as possible. When hungry as we were, I always say that chicken and boiled bacon, with the cabbage cooked with the bacon and flanked by good boiled potatoes, takes a lot of beating; and whatever else the hotel in Buttevant lacked it certainly wasn't food or a cook to cook it. It was just plain roasts and boils, and always cooked to the fraction of a second; you really can't ask more, except a digestion sufficiently amicable to deal with the situation.

I had never been to Cahirmee Fair before and I was anxious to go out and have a look round. Accordingly, having lunched heartily I sauntered out. Naturally, as it was the day before, there wasn't anything to see except the field of battle-to-be. Buttevant is really just a long, straggling village with a very wide road and one or two very small streets off it. I wandered down the street and came to the conclusion that it consisted chiefly of small grocers and general shops, and a great many places where you could get a drink; in fact, it seemed an ideal place to have a horse fair, for, as everyone knows, it takes many drinks to have a deal over a horse, and a few more to clinch it, with the odd spot or two while the cheque is being made out.

Talking of cheques reminds me that it is a very curious thing, but perfectly true, that you can buy a horse in Ireland from a man you have never seen before and who has never seen you; you give him a cheque and take hold of the halter and the deal's done. I regret to say that I do not think I should be so trusting; on selling a horse I like to have the cheque honoured or well recommended before I hand over the halter. The only thing I can think is that as soon as people land in Ireland a sort of awful halo of honesty descends on them and they buy nothing they can't pay for, otherwise surely by now the Irishman would have become wary?

Being, as I fancy I have mentioned before, somewhat on the long and thin side, I created quite a mild sensation in an otherwise slumbering village. I was first discovered by a small girl of about four years old who was having a perfectly delightful time all on her own in the middle of the road. On catching sight of me she unloosed a sort of wail, like a lost soul. This evidently meant something quite definite to her mother, who appeared at a door about twenty yards away. She gave one look, realized at once on seeing me that her daughter had been quite right in summoning her, and at once passed the glad news to someone in the house. The someone at once came out and had a look at me, and strolled off down the road to spread the rumour further. By the time I had got to the bottom of the street, most of the doorways were filled with sightseers and a small but select crowd of children followed in my wake.

Now I don't think I'm really very shy, nor am I as a rule self-conscious, but that was the most terrible journey back up the street. No one jeered, nor apparently stared—the Irish are far too polite for that; they just looked at everything in the street except me. I, not to be outdone in courtesy, also tried to appear as if I didn't realize they had all come out to have a look at me. I was quite extraordinarily glad to arrive back at the hotel and go to ground there. I at once ordered myself an extremely large whiskey to steady my nerves. I was telling a few of the dealers the truly harrowing experience I had had, and the maid, who had been listening, said, ''Twould be the legs on you they were looking at, I never see longer meself.' She then beamed on me and continued on her way.

To be a successful dealer in horse-flesh there are several things you must be. First, it is essential that you should have a head for strong liquor; secondly, it is a great asset to be able to lie with ease and fluency; and thirdly, if buying, you must be able to value a horse quickly, make up your mind what it is worth to you and stick to it. Nothing will deplete your bank account quicker than springing that other 'tenner' just because the horse has taken your fancy. It doesn't matter if you are buying for yourself, but if you are buying to sell again it's very often the aforesaid tenner which makes all the difference between profit and 'just got out'.

The evening before a fair is generally quiet, everyone having made up his mind that whatever has happened before, never again will he indulge in much whiskey before buying horses, but wait till afterwards and then take a nice drink. We dined and talked and went early to bed, as having travelled most of the previous night we were dog-tired. Next morning, having been aroused and seeing the sun shining (a somewhat unusual thing in Ireland, at least it always seems to be raining when I'm there) I decided on a really bold stroke. I decided to take a bath.

I knew there was no hot water because there wasn't even a hot-water tap, and I'm not very fond of plunging my shrinking body into cold water in the early hours of the morning—in fact I know of few more unpleasant things. I therefore sallied forth rather like the knights of old, with a bold front and possibly a sinking feeling inside. There was no lock on the door but that was a mere detail. However, there was one very obvious crab to the whole proceedings, and that was there was no stop to put in the waste-pipe to stop the water running away. I therefore let out a yell for Mary Kate and, on her arriving, explained the situation to her. We searched most diligently for the missing stop but couldn't find it and I, secretly delighted because now I literally couldn't have a cold bath, said: 'Well, it can't be helped; obviously as the water runs away as soon as it runs in I must just wash in my room.' Mary Kate, however, was made of sterner stuff than this and replied: 'Would I put my hand over the hole whilst your honour gets in?'

This kind invitation I refused, however. I'm no Adonis in a bathing dress and I did not feel I should look my best if anyone chanced to come in, happily splashing about in the water while Mary Kate knelt with her hand over the waste.

I think one of the things that probably strikes you most

about an Irish fair is the way the horses and colts are brought in. It's a very common sight to see really high-class colts, who would fetch up to a hundred and sixty pounds and more, being towed in by a halter behind a cart—and, more often than not, getting loose several times on the way into the bargain. From early in the morning they start coming— some led, some ridden and others driven in; all sorts, kinds and conditions and all ages. As a rule the best colts are lodged in yards, pushed into any old place in any old way. I remember seeing a four-year-old sold for just on two hundred pounds to a big dealer, and the only fly in the ointment appeared to be how to get him out of the hovel or pigsty they had put him in while the deal was being finished. The door-was was so low that it did not appear possible that the colt could ever come out, and if I had not seen him in there myself I wouldn't have believed he could ever have been induced to go in. They eventually solved the problem by one of them hanging on to his ears to get his head down while a few trusted friends pushed and heaved from behind.

There are certain men called 'guinea hunters', and they make their living by going from fair to fair and it is their job to make the deal. There is no auction, the horses are sold by the vendor to the customer direct, and you will be a very clever man if you succeed in bringing off a deal without a guinea hunter coming in. Whatever you pay, be it ten pounds or four hundred, their fee is the same, a guinea. No deal, no fee. Let us imagine you have just breakfasted and are strolling down the street, just going to have a look round. I'll guarantee you won't take twenty steps before three or four guinea hunters have a race for you; first man to arrive claims you as his property.

'What will your honour be buying—is it a colt ye'd be looking for, or a great bit of a blood horse, sound, and one that knows leppin' and hounds since he was foaled? Maybe it's one that isn't just right of his wind, or a slight halt in his trot on, that your honour could do with?'

It will save you a lot of time if you make up your mind to pay the guinea, you will have to sooner or later and on the whole the guinea hunter is on your side mostly, as if you don't buy they don't get anything. You can be sure that they have been up before it is light making a note of the horses and colts coming in, and they can take you straight away to see what it's quite possible you would never have found on your own.

Let us suppose it's a horse five or six years old you want. You tell your guinea hunter what you wish to buy, and you might add: 'Mind, the price must be right, I'm not Mr Oliver Dixon and can't afford what he would pay if he liked one.' You set out and eventually find one that you like, five years old, sound (or apparently so), well bred and up to a bit of weight, and you decide to give up to a hundred and eighty for him. On inquiring the price you will be sure to be asked two hundred and fifty, probably more. The correct answer to this is that it's the horse you want to buy, not the bit of a farm as well. With anything like luck at the end of an hour you will have got within striking distance, you having bid a hundred and fifty as your last word and he saying not a penny less would he take than two hundred. The preliminary skirmishing being finished, you then say: 'Well, I'll put a leg over him and see what he's like, but I shan't give another sixpence more than I said.' This is the moment when the guinea hunter girds up his loins, takes a deep breath and wades straight into the battle.

'Throw your leg over him, your honour, try him on the road and if he rides aisy and if he's to your liking we'll take him to the field and gallop and jump him and while you do be riding him I'll spake to the man.' I ought to explain here that 'taking him to the field' means that you go to the nearest field, the gate of which is locked, you pay half a crown, the gate is then unlocked by the owner and you can gallop and jump as much as you like. The field owners round a fair make a very good thing out of it. Having ridden about a bit and found that you like the horse, you return once more to the field of battle and say the horse is a very disappointing ride and you really don't think you will buy him; still, you had mentioned a hundred and fifty and you don't like to go back on your word, so if his owner would jump him over a bank or two you would stand word at a hundred and fifty, though God knows what you would lose over the deal.

You all adjourn therefore to the field and his owner proceeds to hurl him over every bank he can see and a good many you can't. You come to the conclusion that he's a very brave man and the horse a very good performer. The moment has now arrived to say to the guinea hunter, 'I'll buy at a price, what's the lowest he'll take?' You then gather that the horse can be bought for a hundred and ninety. You reply that a hundred and seventy is your outside figure and the matter is left over till the return of the horse and his owner. The amount of time you have to wait usually depends on the amount of drink the lad has had. If a fairish whack he'll very likely go on riding for some time, thoroughly enjoying himself. On his return you hop up yourself and walk about till the horse has got his wind back and then, just as a salve to your own conscience, you possibly jump the smallest bank you can see, gallop him for his wind, return, and then commence on the final round with the horse's owner. A small boy invariably appears at this moment to hold the horse; he hasn't been there till now, whether he springs from the ground or drops out of the clouds I can't say but he always materializes at the psychological moment. You then repair to some haunt known to the guinea hunter where you drink 'Poteen', which is illicitly distilled whiskey, perfectly excellent, goes down like milk and can reduce you to a state of drunkenness sooner than any other drink I have ever competed with.

The remainder of the deal varies first as to the length of your patience, secondly, on how much whiskey it takes to reduce the seller to the state when he ceases to remember exactly how much he originally asked. Backwards and forwards wages the battle. Sometimes the guinea hunter loses his temper with the seller and calls him the most appalling names, but eventually it's completed and at once everyone becomes bosom friends. The guinea hunter takes his guinea, the man takes his cheque, you take hold of the halter and everything is lovely. I can honestly say that if you have a lot of horses to buy, a day in an Irish fair is as hard work as any man can wish for.

Once the fair has started, lasting one, two or three days as the case may be, there are no regular hours for meals at the hotel. Food is always ready at any moment of the day or night. You dash in, and eat, very likely continuing the deal through the window at the same time.

I remember one splendid fellow who was selling a horse to Palmer, and we had got to the stage where we were to adjourn to the field. A small boy by the name of Mick was riding the horse. When we got there we could not find the man to unlock the gate. The field was divided from the road by a wall about three foot six inches high, with a foot drop into the field. Mick was at once ordered to lep the horse into the field, which he did. The deal completed, Palmer was going to look for the man to unlock the gate and let us out, thinking four foot six of stone wall on to a road plenty enough for a horse he had just bought. The owner, however, had other ideas on the subject. 'Let drive at it, Mick,' he yelled. 'What sort of a horse is it that can jump into a field if he can't jump out?' And I'm bound to say he did this extremely well.

This is the sort of thing which goes on the whole time; it's most amusing. Sometimes a deal will start on the first day and you cannot come to terms, and it will go on, on and off all the three days of the fair till eventually, if no one steps in in the meantime, you probably buy the horse at your figure on the last day. There's one thing certain, the Irishman means to sell. There is nothing upsets him more than not having a deal.

Everything and everybody is accommodating there, even the trains. I've seen a train stop at a station while a horse was galloped for his wind up the road, nobody more interested in the deal than the engine-driver. The deal was completed and the horse boxed, the train shunted and off we went. Time to the Irishman is very much like what it was to a certain charabanc conductor who I once asked what the time was. 'Time, time? I don't know,' said he. 'Time means nothing to me.'

(From *Huic Holloa!*)

The White Knight on Equitation

BY LEWIS CARROLL

WHENEVER the horse stopped (which it did very often), he fell off in front; and whenever it went on again (which it generally did rather suddenly) he fell off behind. Otherwise he kept on pretty well, except that he had a habit of now and then falling off sideways; and as he generally did this on the side on which Alice was walking, she soon found that it was the best plan not to walk *quite* close to the horse.

'I'm afraid you've not had much practice in riding,' she ventured to say, as she was helping him up from his fifth tumble.

The Knight looked very much surprised and a little offended at the remark. 'What makes you say that?' he asked as he scrambled back into the saddle, keeping hold of Alice's hair with one hand, to save himself from falling over on the other side.

'Because people don't fall off quite so often when they've had much practice.'

'I've had plenty of practice,' the Knight said very gravely. 'Plenty of practice!'

Alice could think of nothing better to say than 'Indeed?' but she said it as heartily as she could. They went on a little way in silence after this, the Knight with his eyes shut, muttering to himself, and Alice watching anxiously for the next tumble.

'The great art of riding,' the Knight suddenly began in a loud voice, waving his right arm as he spoke, 'is to keep——' Here the sentence ended as suddenly as it had begun, as the Knight fell heavily on the top of his head exactly in the path where Alice was walking. She was quite frightened this time, and said in an anxious voice as she picked him up: 'I hope no bones are broken?'

'None to speak of,' the Knight said, as if he didn't mind breaking two or three of them. 'The great art of riding, as I was saying, is—to keep your balance properly. Like this, you know——'

He let go the bridle and stretched out both his arms to show Alice what he meant, and this time he fell flat on his back, right under the horse's feet.

'Plenty of practice,' he went on repeating, all the time that Alice was getting him on his feet again. 'Plenty of practice.'

'It's too ridiculous,' cried Alice, losing all her patience this time. 'You ought to have a wooden horse on wheels, that you ought!'

'Does that kind go smoothly?' the Knight asked in a tone of great interest, clasping his arms round the horse's neck as he spoke, just in time to save himself from tumbling off again.

'Much more smoothly than a live horse,' Alice said, with

a little scream of laughter, in spite of all she could do to prevent it.

'I'll get one,' the Knight said thoughtfully to himself. 'One or two—several.'

(From *Alice Through the Looking Glass*)

The First Ride

AND it came to pass that, as I was standing by the door of
the barrack stable, one of the grooms came out to me, saying,
'I say, young gentleman, I wish you would give the cob a
breathing this fine morning.'

'Why do you wish me to mount him?' said I. 'You know
he is dangerous. I saw him fling you off his back only a few
days ago.'

'Why, that's the very thing, master. I'd rather see anybody
on his back than myself. He does not like me, but, to them
he does, he can be as gentle as a lamb.'

'But suppose,' said I, 'that he should not like me?'

'We shall soon see that, master,' said the groom; 'and, if
so be he shows temper, I will be the first to tell you to get
down. But there's no fear of that; you have never angered

or insulted him, and to such as you, I say again, he'll be as
gentle as a lamb.'

'And how came you to insult him,' said I, 'knowing his
temper as you do?'

'Merely through forgetfulness, master. I was riding him
about a month ago, and having a stick in my hand, I struck
him, thinking I was on another horse, or, rather, thinking
of nothing at all. He has never forgiven me, though before
that time he was the only friend I had in the world; I should
like to see you on him, master.'

'I should soon be off him. I can't ride.'

'Then you are all right, master. There's no fear. Trust him
for not hurting a young gentleman, an officer's son who can't
ride. If you were a blackguard dragoon, indeed, with long
spurs, 'twere another thing; as it is, he'll treat you as if he
were the elder brother that loves you. Ride! He'll soon teach
you to ride, if you leave the matter with him. He's the best
riding master in all Ireland, and the gentlest.'

The cob was led forth; what a tremendous creature. I had
frequently seen him before, and wondered at him; he was
barely fifteen hands, but he had the girth of a metropolitan
dray-horse, his head was small in comparison with his immense neck, which curved down nobly to his wide back. His
chest was broad and fine, his shoulders models of symmetry
and strength. He stood well and powerfully upon his legs,
which were somewhat short. In a word, he was a gallant
specimen of the genuine Irish cob, a species at one time not
uncommon, but at the present day nearly extinct.

'There!' said the groom, as he looked at him, half-admir-
ingly, half-sorrowfully. 'With sixteen stone on his back, he'll
trot fourteen miles in one hour; with your nine stone, some
two and a half more, ay, and clear a six-foot wall at the end
of it.'

'I'm half afraid,' said I. 'I'd rather you would ride him.'

'I'd rather so too, if he would let me; but he remembers
the blow. Now, don't be afraid, young master, he's longing

to go out himself. He's been trampling with his feet these three days, and I know what that means; he'll let anybody ride him but myself, and thank them; but to me he says, "No! you struck me."'

'But,' said I, 'where's the saddle?'

'Never mind the saddle; if you are ever to be a frank rider, you must begin without a saddle; besides, if he felt a saddle, he would think you don't trust him, and leave you to yourself. Now, before you mount, make his acquaintance—see there, how he kisses you and licks your face, and see how he lifts his foot—that's to shake hands. You may trust him—now you are on his back at last; mind how you hold the bridle—gently, gently! It's not four pair of hands like yours can hold him if he wishes to be off. Mind what I tell you—leave it all to him.'

Off went the cob at a slow and gentle trot, too fast and rough, however, for so inexperienced a rider. I soon felt myself sliding off, the animal perceived it too, and instantly stood stone still till I had righted myself; and now the groom came up: 'When you feel yourself going,' said he, 'don't lay hold of the mane, that's no use; mane never yet saved man from falling, no more than straw from drowning; it's his sides you must cling to with your calves and feet, till you learn to balance yourself. That's it, now abroad with you; I'll bet my comrade a pot of beer that you'll be a regular rough-rider by the time you come back.'

And so it proved; I followed the directions of the groom, and the cob gave me every assistance. How easy is riding, after the first timidity is got over, to supple and youthful limbs; and there is no second fear. The creature soon found that the nerves of his rider were in proper tone. Turning his head half round he made a kind of whining noise, flung out a little foam, and set off.

In less than two hours I had made the circuit of Devil's Mountain, and was returning along the road, bathed with perspiration, but screaming with delight; the cob laughing in his equine way, scattering foam and pebbles to the left and right, and trotting at the rate of sixteen miles an hour.

Oh, that ride! that first ride!—most truly it was an epoch in my existence; and I still look back to it with feelings of longing and regret. People may talk of first love—it is a very agreeable event, I dare say—but give me the flush, and triumph, and glorious sweat of a first ride, like mine on the mighty cob. My whole frame was shaken, it is true; and during one long week I could hardly move foot or hand; but what of that? By that one trial I had become free, as I may say, of the whole equine species. No more fatigue, no more stiffness of joints, after that first ride round the Devil's Hill on the cob.

(From *Lavengro*)

Mr Pickwick as a Horseman

BY CHARLES DICKENS

'Bless my soul!' said Mr Pickwick, as they stood upon the pavement while the coats were being put in. 'Bless my soul! Who's to drive? I never thought of that.'

'Oh! you, of course,' said Mr Tupman.

'Of course,' said Mr Snodgrass.

'I!' exclaimed Mr Pickwick.

'Not the slightest fear, sir,' interposed the hostler. 'Warrant him quiet, sir; a hinfant in arms might drive him.'

'He don't shy, does he?' inquired Mr Pickwick.

'Shy, sir? He wouldn't shy if he was to meet a vaggin-load of monkeys with their tails burnt off.'

The last recommendation was indisputable. Mr Tupman and Mr Snodgrass got into the bin; Mr Pickwick ascended to his perch, and deposited his feet on a floor-clothed shelf, erected beneath it for that purpose.

'Now, shiny Villiam,' said the hostler to the deputy hostler, 'give the gen'l'm'n the ribbins.' 'Shiny Villiam'— so called, probably, from his sleek hair and oily countenance —placed the reins in Mr Pickwick's left hand; and the upper hostler thrust a whip into his right.

'Wo-o!' cried Mr Pickwick, as the tall quadruped evinced a decided inclination to back into the coffee-room window.

'Wo-o!' echoed Mr Tupman and Mr Snodgrass, from the bin.

'Only his playfulness, gen'l'm'n,' said the head hostler encouragingly. 'Just kitch hold on him, Villiam.' The deputy restrained the animal's impetuosity, and the principal ran to assist Mr Winkle in mounting.

'T'other side, sir, if you please.'

'Blowed if the gen'l'm'n worn't a-gettin' up on the wrong side,' whispered a grinning post-boy to the inexpressibly gratified waiter.

Mr Winkle, thus instructed, climbed into his saddle, with about as much difficulty as he would have experienced in getting up the side of a first-rate man-of-war.

'All right?' inquired Mr Pickwick, with an inward presentiment that it was all wrong.

'All right,' replied Mr Winkle faintly.

'Let 'em go,' cried the hostler. 'Hold him in, sir,' and away went the chaise, and the saddle horse, with Mr Pickwick on the box of the one, and Mr Winkle on the back of the other, to the delight and gratification of the whole inn yard.

'What makes him go sideways?' said Mr Snodgrass in the bin, to Mr Winkle in the saddle.

'I can't imagine,' replied Mr Winkle. His horse was drifting up the street in the most mysterious manner—side first, with his head towards one side of the way, and his tail towards the other.

Mr Pickwick had no leisure to observe either this or any

other particular, the whole of his faculties being concentrated in the management of the animal attached to the chaise, who displayed various peculiarities, highly interesting to a bystander, but by no means equally amusing to anyone seated behind him. Besides constantly jerking his head up in a very unpleasant and uncomfortable manner, and tugging at the reins to an extent which rendered it a matter of great difficulty for Mr Pickwick to hold them, he had a singular propensity for darting suddenly every now and then to the side of the road, then stopping short, and then rushing forwards for some minutes, at a speed which it was wholly impossible to control.

'What *can* he mean by this?' said Mr Snodgrass, when the horse had executed his manœuvre for the twentieth time.

'I don't know,' replied Mr Tupman. 'It *looks* very like shying, don't it?' Mr Snodgrass was about to reply, when he was interrupted by a shout from Mr Pickwick.

'Wo-o!' said that gentleman, 'I have dropped my whip.'

'Winkle,' said Mr Snodgrass, as the equestrian came trotting up on the tall horse, with his hat over his ears, and shaking all over, as if he would shake to pieces, with the violence of the exercise. 'Pick up the whip, there's a good fellow.' Mr Winkle pulled at the bridle of the tall horse till he was black in the face; and having at length succeeded in stopping him, dismounted, handed the whip to Mr Pickwick, and grasping the reins, prepared to remount.

Now whether the tall horse, in the natural playfulness of his disposition, was desirous of having a little innocent recreation with Mr Winkle, or whether it occurred to him that he could perform the journey as much to his own satisfaction without a rider as with one, are points upon which, of course, we can arrive at no definite and distinct conclusion. By whatever motives the animal was actuated, certain it is that Mr Winkle has no sooner touched the reins than he slipped them over his head, and darted backwards to their full length.

'Poor fellow,' said Mr Winkle soothingly. 'Poor fellow—good old horse.' The poor fellow was proof against flattery; the more Mr Winkle tried to get nearer him, the more he sidled away; and, notwithstanding all kinds of coaxing and wheedling, there were Mr Winkle and the horse going round and round each other for ten minutes, at the end of which time each was at precisely the same distance from the other as when they first commenced—an unsatisfactory sort of thing under any circumstances, but particularly so in a lonely road, where no assistance can be procured.

'What am I to do?' shouted Mr Winkle, after the dodging had been prolonged for a considerable time. 'What am I to do? I can't get on him.'

'You had better lead him till we come to a turnpike,' replied Mr Pickwick from the chaise.

'But he won't come!' roared Mr Winkle. 'Do come and hold him.'

Mr Pickwick was the very personation of kindness and humanity; he threw the reins on the horse's back, and having descended from his seat, carefully drew the chaise into the hedge, lest anything should come along the road, and stepped back to the assistance of his distressed companion, leaving Mr Tupman and Mr Snodgrass in the vehicle.

The horse no sooner beheld Mr Pickwick advancing towards him with the chaise whip in his hand, than he exchanged the rotary motion in which he had previously indulged, for a retrograde movement of so very determined a character, that it at once drew Mr Winkle, who was still at the end of the bridle, at a rather quicker rate than fast walking, in the direction from which they had just come. Mr Pickwick ran to his assistance, but the faster Mr Pickwick ran forward, the faster the horse ran backward. There was a great scraping of feet, and kicking up of the dust; and at last Mr Winkle, his arms being nearly pulled out of their sockets, fairly let go his hold. The horse paused, stared, shook his head, turned round, and quietly trotted home to

Rochester, leaving Mr Winkle and Mr Pickwick gazing on each other with countenances of blank dismay. A rattling noise at a little distance attracted their attention. They looked up.

'Bless my soul!' exclaimed the agonized Mr Pickwick, 'there's the other horse running away!'

It was but too true. The animal was startled by the noise, and the reins were on his back. The result may be guessed. He tore off with the four-wheeled chaise behind him, and Mr Tupman and Mr Snodgrass in the four-wheeled chaise. The heat was a short one. Mr Tupman threw himself into the hedge, Mr Snodgrass followed his example, the horse dashed the four-wheeled chaise against a wooden bridge, separated the wheels from the body, and the bin from the perch; and finally stood stock still to gaze upon the ruin he had made.

The first care of the two unspilt friends was to extract their unfortunate companions from their bed of quickset—a process which gave them the unspeakable satisfaction of discovering that they had sustained no injury, beyond sundry rents in their garments, and various lacerations from the brambles. The next thing to be done was to unharness the horse. This complicated process having been effected, the party walked slowly forward, leading the horse among them, and abandoning the chaise to its fate.

(From *Pickwick Papers*)

The Colonel's Cup

BY SIEGFRIED SASSOON

THE first two races were little more than the clamour and
commotion of a passing procession. The 'Open Race' was
the main excitement of the afternoon; it was run 'in colours',
and there were about a dozen dashing competitors, several
of them well-known winners in such events.

But everything connected with this contest reached me as
though from a long way off, since I was half stupefied by
yawning nervousness. They appeared to be accomplishing
something incredible by galloping round the course. I had
got to do it myself in half an hour; and what was worse,
Dixon was relying on me to put up a creditable performance.
He even expected me to give the others 'a shaking up'.
Stephen had ceased to be any moral support at all: in spite
of his success last year he was nearly as nervous as I was, and

when the field for the Open Race had filed out of the hurdle-guarded enclosure, which did duty as a paddock, he disappeared in the direction of Jerry and I was left to face the future alone.

Also, as far as I knew, my horse hadn't yet arrived, and it was with a new species of alarm that I searched for him after I had seen the race start; the paddock and its environs now looked unfriendly and forsaken.

I discovered my confederates in a quiet corner under a hayrick. They seemed a discreet and unassuming pair, but Dixon greeted me with an invigorative grin. 'I kept him away from the course as long as I could,' he said confidentially; 'he's as quiet as a sheep, but he knows what he's here for; he's staled twice since we got here.' He told me that Mr Gaffikin was about and had been looking for me. 'He says our horse stands a jolly good chance with the going as good as it is.'

I said there was one place, in and out of a lane, where I'd have to be careful.

We then escorted Cockbird to the paddock; by the time we were there and I'd fetched my weight-cloth, the Open Race was over and the spectators were trooping back again. Among them was Mr Gaffikin, who hailed me companionably with: 'Hullo, old chap; jolly sporting of you to be having a ride!' and thereafter took complete charge of me in a most considerate manner, going with me to the weighing tent with the weight-cloth over his arm, while I, of course, carried my saddle.

The winner of the Open Race was weighing in when we arrived, and I stepped diffidently on to the machine immediately after his glorified and perspiring vacation of the seat. Mr. Gaffikin doled out a few leads for me to slip into the leather pouches on the dark blue cloth until I topped the scale at fourteen stone. The Clerk of the Scales, an unsmiling person with a large, sallow face—he was a corn-merchant—verified my name on the card and handed me my number-cloth and armlet; my number was seven; under less exacting conditions I might have wondered whether it was a lucky number, but I was pushed out of the way by Pomfret. Arthur Brandwick (in a grey bowler) was at his elbow, talking nineteen to the dozen; I caught a glimpse of Stephen's serious face; Colonel Hesmon was with him, behaving exactly the same as last year, except that, having already 'given the boy the horse', he could no longer say that he was going to do so if he won the race.

While Dixon was putting the last testing touches to Cockbird's straps and buckles, the little colonel came across to assure me that if Jerry didn't win there was no one he'd rather see first past the judge's wagon than me. He added that he'd taken a lot of trouble in choosing the cup—'very nice goblet shape—got it from Stegman and Wilks—excellent old firm in the "City"'. But his eye wandered away from Cockbird; his sympathies were evidently strongly implicated in Jerry, who was as unperturbed as if he were being put into a brougham to fetch someone from the station.

Near him, Nigel Croplady was fussing around his horse, with quite a crowd round him.

The terrific 'Boots' Brownrigg, of 'the Blues', was puffing a cigarette with apparent unconcern; his black cap was well over his eyes and both hands were plunged into the pockets of a short blue overcoat; from one of the pockets protruded a short cutting whip. His boots were perfection. Spare built and middle-sized, he looked absolutely undefeatable; and if he had any doubts about his own abilities he concealed them well.

Stifling another yawn, I did my best to imitate his demeanour. The bookies were bawling 'Two to one bar one'. Cockbird, stimulated by publicity, now began to give himself the airs of a real restive racehorse, chucking his head about, flattening his ears, and capering sideways in a manner which caused the onlookers to skip hastily out of range of his heels.

'I say, that's a classy-looking quad!' exclaimed a youth who appeared to have purchased the paddock. He consulted his card, and I overheard his companion, as they turned away, saying something about 'his jockey looking a bit green.' 'We'd better back Nigel's horse. They say he'll win for a cert.'

For want of anything else to do at this critical moment I asked Dixon whether he'd put Homeward's half-crown on. He said, 'Yes, sir; Mr Gaffikin's man has just done it for me, and I've got a bit on for myself. *It's a good thing;* they're laying five to one about him. Mr Stephen's horse is at two's.'

Mr Gaffikin chimed in with 'Mikado's a hot favourite. *Two to one on,* all along the line.' Mikado was Croplady's horse.

Mr Gaffikin then tied the strings of my cap in a very tight bow; a bell jangled and a stentorian voice shouted, 'Now, then, gentlemen, I'm going down to the post.' The blue sky suddenly went white; my heart bumped; I felt dazed and breathless. Then Mr Gaffikin's remote voice said, 'Let me give you a leg up, old chap'; I grabbed hold of the reins, lifted an awkward foot, and was lifted airily on to the slippery saddle; Cockbird gave one prance, and then stood still; Dixon was holding him firmly by the head. Pressing my knees into the saddle I overheard Mr Gaffikin's ultimate advice. 'Don't go in front unless you can help it; but *keep well with 'em.*' They both wished me luck and released me to my destiny.

I felt as if I'd never been on Cockbird's back before; everything around me appeared unreal and disconnected from all my previous experience. As I followed Stephen out of the paddock in a sort of equestrian trance I caught sight of his father's face, pale and fixed in its most strenuous expression; his eyes followed his son, on whose departure he was too intent to be able to take in anyone else. We filed through a gate under some trees: 'Gentlemen George' was standing by the gate; he stared up at me as I passed. 'That's the 'oss for my money,' was all that he said, but his measured tone somehow brought me to my senses, and I was able to look about me when we got down to the starting-place.

But even then I was much more a passenger than a resolute rider with his wits about him to 'pinch' a good start. There were seven others. I kept close to Stephen. We lined up uneasily; while the starter (on his dumpy grey cob) was instructing us to keep the red flags on the right and the white flags on the left (which we already knew) I noticed Pomfret (on a well-bred, excitable brown) and Brownrigg (Crop-lady's bright chestnut looking very compact) already stealing forward on the side farthest from him.

When he said 'Go', I went with the others, albeit with no sense of initiative. The galloping hoofs sounded strange. But Cockbird felt strong under me and he flicked over the first fence with level and unbroken stride; he was such a big jumper and so quick over his fences that I had to pull him back after each one in order to keep level with Jerry, who was going his best pace all the way. One of the soldiers (in a top-hat) was making the running with Brownrigg and Pomfret close behind him. At the awkward fifth fence (the one on a bank) Pomfret's horse jumped sideways and blundered as he landed; this caused Pomfret to address him in uncomplimentary language, and at the next obstacle (another awkward one) he ran out to the left, taking one of the soldiers with him. This, to my intense relief, was the last I saw of him. I took it at a place where a hole had been knocked in it in the previous races. The next thing I remember was the brook, which had seemed wide and intimidating when I was on foot and had now attracted a small gathering of spectators. But water-jumps are deceptive things and Cockbird shot over this one beautifully. (Stephen told me afterwards that he'd 'never seen a horse throw such an enormous lep'.)

We went on up a long slope of firm pastureland, and I now became aware of my responsibility; my arms were aching and my fingers were numb and I found it increasingly difficult to avoid taking the lead, for after jumping a couple more fences and crossing a field of light ploughland we soared over a hedge with a big drop and began to go down the other side of the hill. Jerry was outpaced and I was level with Mikado and the Cavalry soldier who had been cutting out the work. As Stephen dropped behind he said, 'Go on, George; you've got 'em stone-cold.'

We were now more than three parts of the way round, and there was a sharp turn left-handed where we entered on the last half-mile of the course. I lost several lengths here by taking a wide sweep round the white flag, which Brownrigg almost touched with his left boot. At the next fence the soldier went head over heels, so it was just as well for me that I was a few lengths behind him. He and his horse were still rolling about on the ground when I landed well clear of them. Brownrigg looked round and then went steadily on across a level and rather wet field which compelled me to take my last pull at Cockbird. Getting on to better ground, I remembered Mr Gaffikin's advice, and let my horse go after him. When I had drawn up to him it was obvious that Cockbird and Mikado were the only ones left in it. I was alone with the formidable Brownrigg. The difference between us was that he was quite self-contained and I was palpitating with excitement.

We were side by side: approaching the fourth fence from the finish he hit his horse and went ahead; this caused Cockbird to quicken his pace and make his first mistake in the race by going too fast at the fence. He hit it hard and pecked badly; Brownrigg, of course, had steadied Mikado for the jump after the quite legitimate little piece of strategy which so nearly caused me to 'come unstuck'. Nearly, but not quite. For after my arrival at Cockbird's ears his recovery tipped me half-way back again and he cantered on across the next field with me clinging round his neck. At one moment I was almost in front of his chest. I said to myself, 'I *won't*

fall off', as I gradually worked my way back into the saddle.
My horse was honestly following Mikado, and my fate depended on whether I could get into the saddle before we
arrived at the next fence. This I just succeeded in doing,
and we got over somehow, I then regained my stirrups and
set off in urgent pursuit.

After that really remarkable recovery of mine, life became
lyrical, beatified, ecstatic, or anything else you care to call
it. To put it tersely, I just galloped past Brownrigg, sailed
over the last two fences, and won by ten lengths. Stephen
came in a bad third. I also remember seeing Roger Pomfret
ride up to Jaggett in the paddock and inform him in a most
aggressive voice that he'd got to 'something well pay up
and look pleasant'.

Needless to say that Dixon's was the first face I was aware
of; his eager look and the way he said 'Well done' were
beyond all doubt the quintessence of what my victory meant
to me. All else was irrelevant at that moment, even Stephen's
unselfish exultation and Mr Gaffikin's loquacious enthusiasm.
As for Cockbird, no words could ever express what we felt
about him. He had become the equine equivalent of Divin-
ity.

Excited as I was, an inward voice cautioned me to control
my volubility. So when I had weighed in and returned with
my saddle to find a cluster of knowing ones casting an eye
over the winner, I just waited soberly until Dixon had rubbed
him down, mounted, and ridden serenely out of sight. The
colonel was on the spot to congratulate me on my 'nailing
good performance' and, better still, to give Dixon his due
for having got Cockbird so fit. Those few lofty minutes when
he was making much of his horse were Dixon's reward for
all the trouble he had taken since Cockbird had been in his
charge. He had needed no such incentive, but he asked for
nothing more. While he was on his way back to Downfield
he may also have thought to himself how he had made me
into a good enough rider to have got round the course with-

out a catastrophe. (He had yet to hear full details of the race —including my peculiar acrobatics towards the end, which had been witnessed by no one except the rider of Mikado, who had been kind enough to tell Croplady that he never saw such a thing in his life, which was, I hoped, intended as a compliment.)

When I had watched Dixon's departure I found that public interest was being focused on the Yeomanry Team Race. I was glad to slip away by myself: a few fields out in the country I relaxed my legs on a five-barred gate and contemplated my achievement with as much mental detachment as I could muster. Even in those days I had an instinct for getting the full flavour of an experience. Perhaps I was fortunate in not yet having become aware that the winner of the last race is forgotten as soon as the next one starts.

(From *Memoirs of a Fox-Hunting Man*)

The Christening of Hildebrand

BY JOHN THORBURN

ONCE upon a time a black and white horse arrived at Yew Tree Cottage. *How* he arrived or *why* he arrived nobody knew: there was just an empty stable one evening, and the next morning he was there, and looking very innocent, too. They did their best to find his owner and they advertised in *Horse and Hound*, *The Circus Times* and the *Livestock Journal* —'Fnd. blk. & w. hrs. Onr. apy. Box 371'; but nobody answered so they decided to keep him. The first bother was that they didn't know what to call him, and when they *asked* him his name he merely put his near foré hoof to his lips and shook his head to show that he couldn't talk.

They tried a lot of names. 'Whiskey' seemed a good idea for a black and white horse, so they put him in a field and called out 'Whiskey!' But he paid no attention at all. 'Night and Day' was no good either; and then one morning, when they had almost given up hope, they saw the following item of news in the *Dail Wail.*

AMAZING ADVENTURE TO FAMOUS GENERAL

We learn that General MacGarter, an equestrian of considerable repute in modern schools of horsemanship, was discovered at a late hour last night hanging face downwards from the branch of a tree, suspended by his braces. It transpired later that the unfortunate officer had been hanging there since Saturday last—his horse, whom he had always regarded as a trusted friend and willing co-operator, having shied at a firefly and deposited him there. We understand that the General is going on as well as can be expected, but that the horse has gone on so far that he can't be found at all.

And in the *Art Supplement* they saw a heading 'Hildebrand', and under it the following poem:

> *A horse half black and half white,*
> *Has been missing since Saturday night.*
> *His absence though sad*
> *if continued will add*
> *To the owner's eternal delight.*

This looked very suspicious, so they went to the new horse's box and said: 'Is your name by any chance Hildebrand?' And when he heard this, the black and white horse blushed very red, so that the white parts of him became chestnut. But at the same time he saw that he would have to admit that he really was Hildebrand, so he nodded his head while he pretended to be very engrossed in his manger.

Well, after much deliberation, they decided it was no good sending him back to General MacGarter who didn't want him now that he had ceased to be a willing co-operator; and as the black and white horse seemed perfectly happy where he was, they thought he had better stay there.

But the first thing they had to arrange was a christening, because *all* the animals at Yew Tree Cottage were named as soon as ever they arrived. So they sent out the following letter to all the other animals:

On May the twenty second or in other words on Monday,
At the Stables, Yew Tree Cottage, Master Hildebrand requests
The presence of Napoleon with Bonaparte and Sundae
And all the Berkshire Tamworths in their spotted undervests.

At two-fifteen the christening of Hildebrand begins.
A collection will be made so don't forget to bring donations;
And then we'll sing a song of thanks, because he wasn't twins.
All friends are welcome at the Yard, and one or two relations.

The day of the ceremony arrived, and it was a very important occasion for everybody. All the animals were there. Napoleon, and even Bonaparte, had been specially shaved, and Sundae brought the pony cart containing Hush-Hush, Now-Now and Come-Come Tamworth—who were *Berkshire* Tamworths, you must not forget. (Napoleon and Bonaparte were two French poodles, though Bonaparte wasn't really a proper poodle because he used to get rheumatism so it wasn't safe to cut patterns on him; in fact so many people mistook him for a retriever that he was called a Retroodle. Sundae was a pony, not much bigger than a St Bernard dog, and the Berkshire Tamworths were three little pigs, brown ones with funny black spots all over them. They were christened Hush-Hush, Now-Now and Come-Come because that is what nurse would have said if she had heard them eating.)

There were three fairy horse-godmothers, two good and one bad, and they all came to give presents to Hildebrand, each in their turn.

One of the good ones came first, but she was so good that

she always thought of some reason why her presents wouldn't be the right thing to give (especially when they were rather expensive presents); and so at the last minute she usually decided to give something cheaper instead. She first of all thought of 'Happiness', but she said it was well known that a certain amount of unhappiness is good for the character, so she thought again and thought of 'Beauty'; but she decided that a present like that might make Hildebrand vain. So she thought again very hard, and said she had suddenly thought of sixpence. And as she had found one in the road on her way to the party, she gave that to Hildebrand and told him that as long as he kept this sixpence in his purse, he would never be without money. Then she went away very pleased with herself because she had got off so cheaply.

The other good fairy godmother was not quite so good as the first one, but she was much kinder, and she was awfully excited about the present she had brought. When she trotted up the yard to make her presentation there was a very coughy silence. You couldn't hear a pin drop because none of the animals wore pins, but you could easily hear Now-Now Tamworth, who was fast asleep, and snoring in a manner most unbecoming to any Tamworth, let alone a Berkshire Tamworth.

'My gift to Hildebrand,' said the second fairy godmother, coming up, very excited, to little Sundae—who had brought the Tamworths and was looking after Hildebrand—'My gift to Hildebrand is that he shall be able to *talk*. Be able to talk like I do,' she added with a beaming smile, turning to Hildebrand himself.

There was a short pause.

Hildebrand opened his mouth and took a deep breath.

'But,' he said in a terribly loud whisper to little Sundae, 'I don't think she talks very *well*. Besides,' he went on, quite out loud, 'she smiles too much.'

When she heard what a very rude use Hildebrand made of

his nice present, Sundae was very agitated, and she popped into Hildebrand's mouth a carrot which she had brought to keep him quiet in case of emergency. But the fairy godmother who had made him able to talk was more agitated still, because it didn't seem a very good present after all, and because she didn't know what he might say about her next. And she was really specially sorry because there was now only one fairy godmother left. And she was the bad one. In fact, she was a 'Night Mare'.

Now a Night Mare looks simply horrible always, and this one was even worse than usual. Both her eyes were pink, and they crossed each other without giving any warning signal, which was very dangerous; she was jet-black in colour and she never ate anything but hot lobster and toasted cheese. Nobody knew what her name really was but most people called her Sal, which was short for Sal Volatile; this was because she had wings as well as feet. She was terribly common; in fact she was so awfully common that she wore her mane and tail shingled at a time when long manes and tails were fashionable, and she wore her splints in the place where most horses wear spavins. Moreover, she used to bite her manger for forty minutes every day so that her teeth might grow shorter and people think she was younger than she really was. Her heels were very shaggy and when anybody asked her why this was so, she used to say that she grew them like that on purpose, so that they acted as mudguards, and people walking behind her didn't get splashed. This was of course a naughty story because the real reason for her heels being so shaggy was that she was very badly bred.

Now Sal was the kind of horse-godmother who always gives useful presents that people don't want. When Sundae had fallen into a brook while she was out hunting one day, Sal had given her a book about high-diving; and she had given Hush-Hush Tamworth a book on table manners, which was very rude indeed, because, after all, the Berkshire Tamworths don't eat like other people do.

She had thought of a present of this kind for Hildebrand and she was now looking very busy because at last it was her turn. By this time the carrot which Sundae had given him was sticking in Hildebrand's mouth like a cork—so that he *couldn't* speak, and all was quiet again except for Napoleon, who was dreaming rather noisily about one of Bonaparte's favourite bones.

So Sal stepped into the middle of the stable yard to announce her present. What she *meant* to say was, 'Hildebrand shall have lovely thick, curly hair like me'—which at least would have sounded nice and warm; but it was really a rotten present because only cart-horses have thick, curly hair and the better kind of horse makes his owner buy rugs for him, to keep him warm. But the trouble was that, being such a common sort of Night Mare, Sal started off like this:

''Ildebrand shall 'ave . . .'

The carrot came out of Hildebrand's mouth with a loud pop.

'I *beg* your pardon?' he said.

Sal began again:

''Ildebrand shall 'ave . . .'

'Excuse me,' said Hildebrand, 'but——'

Sal was getting very angry at these interruptions, but she tried again.

''Ildebrand shall 'ave . . .'

'Look here,' said Hildebrand, 'I don't want to appear pernickety or anything like that, but I really think I ought to tell you that my name starts with an aitch; Hildebrand, Hildebrand, *Hil*debrand; like that.'

By this time Sal had completely lost her temper.

'Starts with an aitch, does it?' she shouted. '*I'll give you haitches!* I'll give you so many haitches that from now hon heverything you heat shall 'ave to start with a haitch, too. And I 'ope you're 'ungry you hinsolent beast,' she snorted, as she galloped out of the yard in a huff. And as she turned

the corner she was leading with the wrong leg, which just
shows what a frightfully common Night Mare she was.

And after that the christening of Hildebrand ended, and
everybody said it might have been better if Hildebrand had
had two godfathers and only one godmother, like any other
boy; but they had a party that night which was a great
success and lasted well into the early hours of the morning,
and all the animals were very cross at breakfast.

After the ceremony Sundae was asked by all the other
animals if she would continue to look after Hildebrand, so
she said all right and that he could share a stable with her.
But this was not a very satisfactory arrangement because
there was only room for one of them to lie down at a time,
which meant that they had to take it in turns to sleep. And
as Sundae was much older than Hildebrand, she always had
first choice and she always chose the night-time for her turn,
and Hildebrand used to get very bored because he was not
able to read or do anything like that in the dark and he kept
waking Sundae up to ask her what time it was.

But the biggest bother of all was, of course, the problem
about *feeding* Hildebrand, because the Night Mare had made
it impossible for him to eat anything which didn't start with
an *aitch*, and except for hay, nothing at all convenient
seemed to start with an aitch. Hildebrand soon got tired of
hay, and although Sundae used to chop it up and called it
hot-pot, or mince it and call it Hamburg steaks, or even
make it into lumps and call it hash, he soon got used to all
these dodges and always recognized that it was just common
or garden hay.

For a short time Sundae gave him a pair of green spectacles to wear, which made him think he was eating fresh
grass; and occasionally she put magnifying glasses over his
eyes which made him think he was eating macaroni; but he
always discovered in the end that it was nothing but hay,
and he soon began to grow very peevish about it.

One morning, about a month after the christening, things came to a crisis. It was the fifteenth time that Sundae had been disturbed during the night by Hildebrand asking her what the time was, but at last she was able to say:

'Eight o'clock.'

'Time for breakfast,' said Hildebrand. 'What have you got today?'

'Ah!' said Sundae, 'I've got a lovely surprise for you, you can have three guesses.'

'I guess hay, hay, hay,' said Hildebrand, gloomily and immediately. 'Wrong, wrong, wrong,' said Sundae, and she looked very mysterious. Then she went into a corner of the stable and brought out a thing which looked like a football.

'What on earth is that?' exclaimed Hildebrand. 'If it begins with an aitch at all I bet it's a hoax.'

'No,' said Sundae. 'It is something very rare and Scotch and it is called a haggis,' and she took a large spoonful and gave it to him to eat.

Hildebrand chewed it carefully and thoughtfully, and then he looked very hard at Sundae.

'You wicked old woman,' he said, 'this is nothing but minced mouldy hay wrapped up in a nasty old chamois-leather. I shan't stay in this beastly stable for one single day longer.' And he picked up the remainder of the haggis, kicked it in Sundae's face and galloped away into the blue.

Eventually he came to rest in a large field, where the hedges were lovely and thick and looked as if they might contain all kinds of surprising things that started with aitch. But the most thrilling part of the whole field was a huge pond which Hildebrand thought must be full of haddocks, herrings and perhaps even halibut (of which he was particularly fond).

But after he had been in the field a week he had eaten all the hips and haws in the hedges, and he was beginning to grow exceedingly hungry. He didn't seem to be able to find the right kind of worms to catch haddocks or herrings or halibuts. The bees were not laying at all well either, so there wasn't any honey, and ham always gave him the hiccups, so he could not have eaten that even if there had been any. And there wasn't.

In the end he tried to eat the hedges themselves, but the prickles used to puncture his tummy every time he took a deep breath.

The farmer who owned the field used to bring him a feed of corn every day, but that wasn't any good because it didn't start with an aitch; so the hens used to eat it instead. Hildebrand did think of eating the hens, but when he managed to catch one of them he got his mouth full of feathers and he didn't like it at all.

And so he got hungrier and hungrier, which pleased Sal Volatile enormously, until one day a most peculiar man walked past the field. He was wearing a very shiny pair of top-boots and very long spurs, his breeches were of a reddish-brown colour and he had a bright check coat. There was an enormous imitation diamond pin in his tie, as big as a decanter stopper. He wore his bowler hat all on one side, and he had a very red face and his name was Horace.

Horace stopped, picked up a straw and put it in his mouth; then he took off his hat, scratched his head, and put his hat back again a little bit more on one side than ever. And then he put his elbows on the gate, his face in his hands, and stared at Hildebrand for a long time.

'Who *are* you?' asked Hildebrand.

'I'm Horace the Horse-Dealer,' replied Horace.

'How many horses have you got?'

'None,' said Horace, 'I'm looking for one.'

'But you can't be a horse-dealer with only one horse,' said Hildebrand.

'Oh yes I can,' said Horace. 'You see, I hire out horses in a one-horse town.'

'I see,' said Hildebrand.

Horace went on staring at him but after a minute or two he spoke again. 'Horse,' he said, 'you are very thin.'

'Yes,' said Hildebrand, who was delighted to have anybody to grumble to. 'I'm an absolute skellington, aren't I?
And I look as if I'd swallowed a toast-rack, don't I? You see
I can only eat things which start with an aitch, and I have
already eaten all the hay, and the hips and haws in the
hedges, and if I try to eat the hens I get my mouth full of
feathers. I am awfully fond of herrings and halibut,' he went
on sadly, 'but I have fished and fished in the pond and the
only things I ever catch are tadpoles and sticklebacks, so
what *is* a horse to do?'

'But look,' said Horace, 'look at the nice feed the farmer
has brought you! Why don't you eat that?'

'Corn doesn't start with an aitch,' sighed Hildebrand.
'Nor do carrots and sugar, worse luck.'

'Do you call it corn?' asked Horace, in surprise. 'Because
I call it hoats.'

A gleam of hope appeared in Hildebrand's eye.

'Do you *always* call it hoats?' he cried. 'Really and truly
always?'

'Absolutely halways,' said Horace, 'and carrots and sugar
I call hextras.'

Hildebrand put his forelegs round Horace's neck and
hugged him.

'Horace,' he said, 'you are the very person I've been waiting for; take me to live with you for halways.' And he proceeded to gobble up the hoats.

'That's all very well,' objected Horace. 'That's all very
well. But I can't just *take* you. Who do you belong to?'

'Well, I used to belong to General MacGarter,' admitted
Hildebrand, 'but I ceased to be a willing co-operator and
he stopped loving me, so I went to live with Sundae. But
then I ceased to be an obedient child and so *she* stopped
loving me, too. So then I ran away by myself and now I don't
think I belong to anybody at all.'

Horace thought for a minute, and suddenly he had a
brainwave.

'You are quite sure they don't love you any more?' he asked.

'Positive,' said Hildebrand. 'They wouldn't have me back at any price. In fact I wouldn't dare to go back unless you gave me a suit of armour.'

'Wait a minute then,' said Horace. 'I must go and telephone.' And he went into the farm.

First of all he rang up General MacGarter.

'Good morning, General,' he said. 'Hi've got an 'orse here called Hildebrand what says he belongs to you—when shall I bring him back?'

'Never,' said a gruff voice at the other end.

'Oh, but I reely *must*, sir,' said Horace; 'you know, sir, you are responsible for the 'orse and he's doing the most frightful damage everywhere. You'll have to pay all the farmers 'undreds and 'undreds of pounds in compensation.'

The voice at the other end began to sound rather nervous. 'I say, could you possibly *drown* Hildebrand for me?' it asked.

'Habsolutely *him*possible,' said Horace. 'But I tell you what I will do, sir—if you give me ten pounds I'll keep him.'

'I'll send you a cheque immediately,' said General MacGarter.

Horace then rang up Sundae.

'Good morning, Sundae,' he said. 'I've found Hildebrand —is it convenient if I bring him back this afternoon?'

'No,' said Sundae.

'When will it be convenient?'

'It won't be.'

'But he's *starving* and the Royal Society for the Prevention of Cruelty to Animals will have you put in prison.'

Sundae sounded rather frightened.

'I say, could you possibly shoot him for me?'

'Habsolutely himpossible,' said Horace, 'But if you will give me a sack of hoats and a bag of carrots and a pound of sugar every week, I'll promise to keep him for you.'

'Right,' said Sundae. 'Call round for the stuff every Monday morning.'

Horace then walked back to the field, where Hildebrand had eaten all the Hoats and was lying on his back with his legs in the air, fast asleep. Horace woke him up.

'Hildebrand,' he said. 'If I take you to live with me and give you plenty of Hoats and Hextras, will you be a good hunter to me?'

'Yes,' said Hildebrand, and went to sleep again. And that is how Hildebrand came to belong to Horace the Horse-Dealer.

(From *Hildebrand*)

Phari the Pony and Thunder the Mule

BY M. E. BUCKINGHAM

ON the next morning, after much haggling, the wool and the mules changed hands, and when, at the end of a week, Ta-Lung started back to Yatung, Hail and Thunder marched side by side at the tail of the caravan. It was not long before Ta-Lung discovered why Hussain had been so anxious to get rid of them, for a worse-tempered pair never wore harness. They had been named after the two most unpopular demonstrations of nature in Tibet, and they did their best to live up to their names. They bit and kicked everyone and everything within reach, or bit and kicked each other if there was nobody else near at hand.

Now Ta-Lung took a pride in the well-being of his animals, an uncommon trait in a Tibetan, and his purchases compared unfavourably in appearance as well as in temper with the rest of the mule-train. However, they were young, and he hoped that with proper care he would soon get them into shape. But a complication arose at the outset.

One morning Ta-Lung's son, Ke-sang, came running to his father with strange news. 'Father! Father!' he cried. 'Phari, my pony, and the new mule, Thunder, are feeding out of the same tin, turn and turn about!'

Ta-Lung looked up at his son in surprise. 'That's curious,' he said. 'Whatever makes them do that?'

Ke-sang had no explanation to offer, and Ta-Lung's surprise increased when, on starting for the day's march, Phari refused to be separated from his new friend. Ta-Lung did his best; the mule was taken to the front of the column time and again in order to keep them apart, but either Thunder succeeded in breaking away, or Phari, regardless of Ke-sang's kicks and blows, pushed his way forward through the mule-train and rejoined his friend. In the end the animals got their own way, and for the sake of peace the mule marched at the head of the caravan half a pace behind Phari. Both beasts seemed perfectly satisfied with this arrangement, and Ta-Lung was highly amused, but Ke-sang felt that his dignity had been lowered, and sulked for several miles of the journey.

The curious friendship formed on that trip proved to be no flash in the pan. Wherever the pony went Thunder went too, or tried to go; if the mule was shut in the barn Phari was unmanageable until he had joined it.

Once Ta-Lung, accompanied by his wife and children, went up the valley to visit some friends. Thunder had been tied up in the barn, and the mutinous Phari, with Ke-sang on his back, was herded like a sheep along the road by members of Ta-Lung's family.

It was a miserable journey for Ke-sang. When they were barely a mile out of Yatung Phari bucked his rider over his head, and promptly bolted back to the village. A furious Ta-Lung and a tearful Ke-sang doubled back after him.

They found Phari where they expected to find him, calmly standing beside the mule, sharing what was left of the pile of grass that had been given to Thunder with the idea of keeping him happy. Thunder had ungratefully kicked most of it to the four winds.

Phari received an even more severe beating than usual; a rope was tied to his bridle, and, the other end held firmly in Ta-Lung's hand, they set out once more.

But the visit was not a success. Phari refused all food, and stood stock-still in the middle of the field whenever he was hobbled and turned out to graze. When they got back to Yatung they found that Thunder had also gone on a food-strike. One of the muleteers was laid up from a kick that he had received, and another had been bitten when he had attempted to muzzle the mule.

Ta-Lung was forced to give in. In future either both beasts went on an expedition or both stayed at home. When they were together there was no trouble; Thunder would carry any load without protest, and Phari never attempted either to throw his rider or give way to panic at some imaginary landslide. In time the odd pair became known throughout the Chumbi Valley, and Ta-Lung began to take pride in owning so queer a couple.

It was not long, however, before Phari began to be famous on his own account, for as he grew older he developed a remarkable turn of speed. Ke-sang, greatly to his joy, was chosen to ride him in the race held during the 'Crop Circuit' festival early in July. It was to be a big race, for the farmers from all the neighbouring villages had entered their ponies.

The day of the feast dawned brightly. Tents for the visitors had been pitched on the waste ground bordering the houses, and everybody gave himself up to enjoyment. The race was to be the first event of the morning; an archery competition followed, and the festival closed in a procession of all the inhabitants with their friends round the fields. This was the 'Crop Circuit', the most important event of the day, for during the procession the peasants offered up prayers for rain while the crops were still green.

Ke-sang was trembling with excitement as he sat on Phari's back waiting for the signal to start. By Ta-Lung's advice Tao-Sang led Thunder close to the starting-point, in case Phari should sulk if he thought that his friend had been left behind.

In order to make doubly sure Ke-sang had tried to explain matters to them on the evening before the race. He had saddled Phari and, standing between the two animals, had poured out his hopes for the morrow.

'Listen, Phari,' he had said. 'Tomorrow I shall ride you in a great race for the honour of the family. You, Thunder, must not try to follow!' Here Ke-sang placed one hand on the mule's nose, gently pushing him backwards, while he pulled Phari forward with the other. 'Thus!'

He jumped upon Phari's back and galloped off round the field; but Thunder promptly galloped after them. Ke-sang dismounted and took Thunder firmly by his halter.

'No, foolish one! I do not mean to deceive you. You would not bring scorn on Phari, would you? Here, Phari, tell him!'

Thunder permitted them to make a short circle without his company, and bit by bit Ke-sang enlarged it, until he could gallop at will as long as he did not get out of Thunder's sight.

Now, as he sat trembling on Phari's back, he wondered whether Thunder would remember the lesson. But he had not long to wonder, for the signal was suddenly given, and he found himself galloping along in a helter-skelter of other ponies. All he could do was to hang on and trust to Phari's strength to shake off his opponents. The pony's mouth was as hard as iron, and Ke-sang, holding on for dear life, was

quite incapable of checking his headlong rush. Phari saw
a gap ahead in the mass of galloping ponies and made for
it; he tore through it as quickly as if half the mountains of
Tibet were crashing down the *khud* behind him. And once
clear he showed that turn of speed for which he was fast
becoming famous.

Even Ta-Lung, who had expected Phari to win, was
amazed that he should shake off the other ponies so soon,
and win so easily. He elbowed his way through the crowd
of people who had surged round the flushed and excited
Ke-sang.

'Excellent!' he said. 'Give him a rub down, and then take
him back to Thunder.'

But Thunder, with a panting small boy in tow, had
already shoved his way to Phari's side, and the pair were
greeting each other as though they had been parted for a
week instead of a few minutes.

Ta-Lung frowned; the result of the race had already con-
firmed him in his intention to sell Phari as a racing pony in
Darjeeling—but who would buy a mule as well? 'I could get
a good price for him,' he mused, 'but will he ever race
without the mule being near at hand? He will lie down and
die as soon as they are separated.'

It was a knotty problem, for who would believe such a
thing possible if he had not seen them together?

Ta-Lung said nothing to Ke-sang of his plans when they
rode to Darjeeling a year later for the race meeting, and
the boy had no idea that he was going to part from his
favourite.

For a year the pony had been rigorously trained whenever
he could be spared from the wool-train, and the hard life
of marching to and fro over the mountain track had strength-
ened his muscles and increased his powers of endurance.

Ta-Lung, as a Tibetan landowner, was qualified to take
part in the race held on the first day of the meeting. Phari

was to be ridden by Ke-sang, and as neither horse nor rider was known in India, Ta-Lung was almost the only person to back him—and he backed him heavily!

By a stroke of luck the Gurkha policeman in charge of the crowd near the starting-point was a friend of his, and no objection was made to Tao-sang's presence at the side of the course with the indispensable Thunder.

Phari had been entered for three races—the stout Bhutia ponies think nothing of running three or four times in an afternoon—and from the start of the first race it was clear that Ta-Lung's judgement was justified.

Phari won the first race with the greatest ease. Obviously a new champion had arrived and the odds against him quickly shortened. In his second race there was no stopping him; a more experienced jockey would have checked him, and allowed him to win with far less effort; as it was, Phari had taken matters out of Ke-sang's hands each time and had galloped all out—for he was as excited as any of the onlookers and Ke-sang was powerless to keep him in check, in spite of Ta-Lung's advice to take things easily.

For the third race—the last but one of the day—Phari started as favourite. But he had overshot his bolt, and went dead lame. The crowd, considering that they had been duped, shouted insults at him as he was pulled up by Ke-sang and led away before he had covered half the course, and Ta-Lung's anger was almost ungovernable—although the money that he had won on the first two races more than made up for his losses on the third. He collected Thunder and Tao-sang and, with a growl to Ke-sang to follow with Phari, set out quickly on the road back to the town in order to get clear before the crowds started pouring down the only road after the race.

They had not gone far when they heard the clattering of a pony's hoofs coming up behind them. They drew into the side of the road to give the rider plenty of room to pass, for Phari was still very excited, and Ta-Lung was afraid of him injuring his sprained muscle. But the rider stopped as he drew level with them.

'Are you Ta-Lung?' he asked, in the hill dialect. 'I am Martin Sahib, from Meshoke tea-garden. They tell me that you are the owner of that pony.'

Ta-Lung stopped and smiled agreeably; it looked as if his luck had not deserted him after all. 'Sahib, that is my name,' he said. 'Did you wish to speak to me?'

'Yes! Yes! But not now, I must get back to the race-course. Can you come up to the Planters' Club this evening about seven?"

Ta-Lung's anger vanished instantly. 'Assuredly, Sahib!' he answered. 'I will be there at seven o'clock.'

As the tea-planter swung his pony round and galloped back the way that he had come, Ke-sang turned cold with apprehension.

'Father! Do you think that he wants to buy Phari?' he asked anxiously.

'I hope so,' answered Ta-Lung shortly. 'Why should I bring the pony to Darjeeling, if not to sell him? Have you not already nearly ruined my chance by your mad riding? And now that our luck has changed again, must you invite the gods' anger by your tears?'—for Ke-sang had started to weep at the thought of losing Phari. 'I will get another pony for you, my son. And you shall win many races.'

'I don't want another pony,' blubbered Ke-sang. 'I want Phari.'

Ta-Lung's wrath rose against the boy, and he cuffed his head. 'Am I to keep a pony that will bring me good money, when I can get another for half the price—and as good?' he shouted. 'Stop crying, and don't be foolish!'

'Maybe I shall get a rupee to spend in the bazaar?' sniffed Ke-sang, intent on getting what he could out of the bargain, for he knew from experience that it was useless to argue with his father.

'If I sell Phari, perhaps you will,' replied Ta-Lung.

Ke-sang consoled himself with this half-promise; he would do his best to make the sahib buy Phari, for, if he did not, some other sahib would, and then he, Ke-sang, might not get his rupee. Accordingly he put on his most engaging air when he presented himself with his father at the Planters' Club that evening.

The signs were propitious, for the sahib looked pleased. Doubtless he had done well at the races that afternoon, and Ke-sang thrust out his tongue at him with a beaming smile.

Mr Martin acknowledged the Tibetan salute cheerfully. He *had* done well that day, and was prepared to pay a good price for the pony that had showed such promise, in spite of the fact that it had gone lame after the second race. He knew that with one of his boys in the saddle Phari would have had enough in hand to win all three races—for he had some experience with Bhutia racing ponies, and he has seldom seen one with such a turn of speed.

'Well, Ta-Lung,' he said, 'what do you want for that pony of yours that went lame this afternoon?'

Ta-Lung was quick to detect an excuse for lowering Phari's value.

'Sahib, it was but an accident,' he answered. 'A slight straining of a muscle—a stone in the hoof—a very small one, but painful. He will be all right by tomorrow.' He raised his hands in the air, as if calling on all the saints in the Buddhist calendar to bear witness to Phari's virtues. 'The pony is swift and well-mannered—you, Sahib, saw how swift. Shall a little stone——'

'Well, well, Ta-Lung, we will not quarrel about the price,' said Mr Martin with a smile, for he knew as well as Ta-Lung that the colt had been overworked. 'How much do you want for him?'

This was excellent so far; Ta-Lung smiled to himself, and hugged his wrists under his long-sleeved coat. 'There is, however, one small difficulty, Sahib,' he said pleasantly.

'What is that?' asked Mr Martin quickly. He wanted the pony badly, and he wondered if, in spite of his promptitude, someone else had been after it.

'The pony cannot be sold without a mule—one Thunder by name,' explained Ta-Lung.

Mr Martin laughed. 'Don't be absurd!' he said. 'Whoever heard of such a thing!'

Ke-sang stepped forward. 'Sahib, it is true!' he exclaimed. 'Did you not see that the mule also was present at the races? Who would take a mule to a race if it was not necessary?'

'Ho! Ho! So the young shaver is in the plot too!' thought Mr Martin to himself. 'There's something queer about this! Surely you do not expect me to believe a story like that?' he added aloud.

'Sahib, you shall see for yourself,' interposed Ta-Lung. 'Take the pony for two days, and leave the mule with me. If the pony does not sulk and refuse his food you need pay me fifty rupees only! If he pines you can send for the mule, and the price for the pair will be three hundred and fifty rupees! I will give you my written word that I will buy back the mule at any time for fifty rupees if you can separate them! See! I do not wish to cheat you!'

Mr Martin was amazed by the strangeness of the offer. 'Come! Come!' he said. 'You can't do that! That pony is worth three hundred rupees to anybody!'

'Sahib, my money is safe. I shall leave Darjeeling this week with three hundred and fifty of your rupees in my purse!' rejoined Ta-Lung, slowly shaking his head with a smile.

Thus did Phari pass that night into the hands of the owner of Meshoke, and two days later the mule Thunder was his property also, for Ta-Lung's prophecy was fulfilled.

Ke-sang, unknown to his father, had two rupees to spend in the bazaar, for Mr Martin had slipped one into his hand when he had led Phari over to the club stables, and taken his last farewell of him. But he did not get a third rupee when later he brought the mule Thunder.

(From *Phari—The Adventures of a Tibetan Pony*)

Melka is Stolen by Gypsies

BY JOAN PENNEY

WHEN darkness had finally settled like a cloak over the countryside, a heavier and more persistent rustling came from the hedge beside the road. Melka pricked her ears, and Telephone the donkey wagged one of his, listening, but before they could plunge into the safe freedom of the paddock two men appeared between them and the blackness of the night.

As one of the men approached her, Melka shrank back and plunged a little; but, undeterred, the man ran one sure hand down her neck and then, as, shivering slightly, she stood still, slipped a halter over her head.

'Got 'er!' he whispered triumphantly, and then, as once before in Khartoum, Melka was led off silently through the night.

Once the halter was over her head she allowed herself to be led quietly enough. At first, Telephone trotted at her heels, but as they reached the gate the second man shooed him away. He scampered off, but when the gate was shut behind Melka and she was led off up the lane, away from the house, and away from him, his anxious cries shattered the night.

'Drat the brute! Hollerin' like that!' muttered the man who was leading Melka, and he cuffed her roughly on the nose as she would have lifted her head to whinny in answer to the cries of her friend.

'It's late,' answered the other. 'No one'll pay any 'eed at this time o' night.'

'Might've bin better to take the cuddy along too!' said the first.

'Then it's you that'd've bin the ass, Davy!' answered the other. 'We'll need to be in luck, and stick to the side roads, to get away with the *gry* at all. An' if we do git caught, we might be able to explain 'er away, like. But if we 'ad the two of 'em . . .' He spat expressively.

'Dessay ye're right!' answered Davy. 'Wish we could've coloured 'er up a bit, though,' he added a moment later.

'No go!' said the other tersely. 'Pedro would smell a rat! I guess he'll stand fer a little shuttin' of an eye, so to speak, but 'e'd feel bound to scratch 'is 'ead a bit if she wer dyed some onnatural colour!'

After that, neither of them spoke for some time as they stumbled along the narrow lane.

'*Dablo!* It's dark!' grumbled Davy as he tripped over a stone.

'Guess we could stick a match to this blarsted lantern now,' said the other, suiting his action to the word.

The faint light of the lantern flickered along the hedges, discovering occasional gleams of hawthorn powdered so thickly with white blossom that it looked as if the hedges were covered with snow. But, for the most part, the shadows

seemed to draw nearer, and, although the lantern illuminated her path, Melka started nervously once or twice when
a blackness in the shadows seemed to move—some dim
memory of a night many years before, when she was lost in
the African bush, stirring in her memory.

'Hey! Give over there!' cursed Davy, as she shied with
a clatter of hoofs at the sharp bark of a dog from a farmhouse
they were passing.

'Ah!' he grunted a moment later, relief in the sound, as a
faint light flickered in the distance: a stationary light, low
to the ground.

They soon reached it; a camp-fire burning outside a low,
rather squalid-looking tent, while in the background looked
a ramshackle cart with a hoop of brown cloth over it, and
a dirty old green caravan, badly in need of a coat of paint,
with a filthy black chimney standing at a crazy angle on
the roof.

'*Dablo!* Come on, there!' stormed the man Davy. 'We
must be gettin' along out of this, or we'll be a darned sight
too near 'ere in the mornin' fer *my* likin'! Ye should've 'ad
that tent stowed long since. Get a move on now, fer goodness
sake!"

At his shouts, a young girl with black, curly hair and a
brown skin came out of the caravan and gave Davy's friend
a hand with the tent, while an old woman and a sleepy-eyed
child peered out at them.

Meanwhile, Davy hitched Melka to a tree, and going off
into the darkness, returned immediately with a bony black
horse. He harnessed this horse quickly, and put him between
the shafts of the van, while another young girl appeared out
of the night, leading a shaggy, piebald pony, which she
harnessed in the cart.

A few moment's bustle, and all was ready. Davy came over
to Melka, unhitched her from the tree, and tied her to the
tail of the caravan.

'It'll be time enough in the morning to put this *gry*

between shafts,' he said. 'Then she'll be less noticeable, like, but jist now, we must get along.'

And so they moved off into the night; the caravan first, with a lantern swinging in front of it and Melka tied behind; then the cart, with another lantern swinging from its tail.

For hours and hours they trudged on. Melka found herself walking in a half-sleep, lulled by the rumbling rhythm of the wagon wheels and the clip-clop of the pony's hoofs behind.

On they went, until the darkness paled to dawn and trees and hedges came to life against the delicate grey of a sky which gradually turned to gold as a myriad birds began to twitter. Still they tramped on, until, when the sun had been up for four hours or more, and the complaining voices of the children could be heard wailing from the wagon, they turned off the road, and following a grassy track which led round a thicket, they plunged into a thick wood.

'Now—no fires this day—an' any *chave* that raises its voice'll get a leatherin' frum me!' said Davy sourly as he untied Melka. 'I don't want no interferin' *gajo* snoopin' around here!'

So saying, he hobbled Melka by tying an old rag round her forelegs, and turned her loose with the black horse and the piebald pony. The horse knelt down and managed to roll, in spite of his hobble, but Melka stood swishing her tail, wondering what had happened to her.

'You're a bit of a star-back, ain't you?' asked the piebald pony, sidling up to Melka.

'Star-back? What's that?' asked Melka in her turn.

'Coo! You don't know much! Star-backs are the posh seats in a circus—all red plush—*you* know!'

'I've never seen a circus!' confessed Melka.

'Coo! You don't know *nuffin*!' said the pony. 'Where *have* you bin brought up?'

For the rest of the day, in the intervals between cropping the sweet, long grass which grew in the woodland glades, and drinking cool draughts from little streams, Melka told the story of her life to the black van horse and the little piebald pony. Then they, in turn, told of their lives; the black horse's bounded by gypsy camps, while the pony had once been half-wild on Exmoor, and from there had spent four years in a circus before he had joined the vagabond gypsy company. Now, tramping the road in sunshine, storms, snow or sleet—neither of them would have exchanged the life for anything but liberty. For real freedom—yes: the freedom the pony had known on Exmoor, or even a lazy life in a paddock: but nothing which meant stables and what they felt to be the cage of routine.

They were still talking when Davy came through the trees, and catching Melka only, led her back to the camp.

Leaving her hobbles on, he proceeded to put the pony's harness on her back. It was small and uncomfortable for her, but she bore with the discomfort and stood quietly enough until Davy pushed her tail through the crupper—then she lashed out.

'Yer wud, wud ye?' threatened Davy coldly, as he hit her across the hocks with the butt of an old whip he was carrying. Melka plunged forward, but the hobbles brought her to her knees. When she had struggled to her feet again and stood trembling, Davy unhobbled her and led her over to the cart.

Although still trembling, she stood still while he pushed the shafts through the harness, so that she felt them pressing against her sides, enclosing her. But when Davy leapt into the cart, and, taking up the reins, touched her with his whip so that she walked forward—then she sprang into terrified, fighting life.

She could feel the cart leaping like a live thing behind her, while the wheels rumbled and growled at her like a wild beast. She careered over the grass, trying to escape, but, try as hard as she could, the pursuing cart racketed and bumped at her heels. Failing in her attempts to plunge away from this terrifying thing, she lashed out at it—and lashed out and lashed out until her heels were bruised and bleeding. And all the time Davy rained blows on her back, her sides, her head, while the cruel lash of his whip curled round her belly, raising sharp little weals on her white coat.

The fight was a short one. Melka was too wise and too kindly at heart to fight long. When her first blind terror had passed, the punishing sting of the whip horrified her friendly soul, and all of a sudden she stopped kicking and stood trembling again.

Then Davy leapt off the cart, and cursing because of the damage she had done, rained blows on her head with one fist, so that she shrank panic-stricken from him again, throwing her head up in terrified jerks, while he held her fast with his other hand. Then, still cursing, he climbed once more into the cart, and this time Melka trotted meekly over the grass, the cart creaking at her heels. And all that night, and for many nights afterwards, she drew the cart behind her over the by-ways of England, while the caravan loomed in front of her and the piebald pony trotted behind.

All through the month of May, avoiding towns and main roads, and travelling mostly by night, the gypsies wandered north.

Melka found trailing along the road a dreary business. Far from sharing the van-horse and piebald pony's love of the vagabond gypsy life, she longed for her comfortable stable, and the feel of Dick in the saddle on her back. She missed the faithful Telephone, too, and her other Woodside Farm friends. Her present companions were friendly enough, but they did not seem to take the edge off her loneliness. As for Davy, though now that she was used to the cart she never again had to submit to the shame and terror of a thrashing such as she had received at her first harnessing, she got many an undeserved cuff from him, and never a friendly pat or word of encouragement.

So it was with a sad heart that she trudged the sleepy,

leafy English lanes, which for the most part wound past lush fields laden with buttercups until, one day, they came to wilder country, where the pony had to be harnessed with ropes in front of the black horse, to help pull the van up steep, stony tracks. Here they had wilder weather, too, and it was on a night of wind and rain, when the storm-tossed trees swished and moaned and the puddles on the road gleamed greyly in the lantern's light, that Melka wearily pulled her ramshackle cart across the little bridge over the Sark, past a yellow disc which bore the name—'Scotland'.

And so, in the middle of a wild, wet night, Melka trailed a tinker's cart through Gretna Green, where on just such a night in olden days, a coach rocking and swaying as the postilions urged on galloping, foam-flecked horses, might have thundered up to the famous blacksmith's shop, so that yet another runaway couple might add their names to the long list of Gretna Green marriages.

For two hours after that, the gypsies battled along in the teeth of the wind, then they camped for what was left of the night in a sandy hollow, among dry, bent grass, on the north shore of the Solway Firth. The gale swept relentlessly over the flats, and wind and sea roared together in Melka's ears on this her first night in Scotland. She stood with her back to the storm, water streaming from her darkened, rain-sodden coat, trying to find some grazing among the tough, salty grasses.

When dawn broke she was still hungry, and very wet and cold in that bleak, unsheltered spot. She was almost thankful when, after an hour or so, Davy came along and threw her harness on, then pushed her between the shafts of the cart. The sodden, too-tight straps were chafing her flanks and quarters, but she was glad to turn her back on the moaning sea, and as they turned north-west the wind seemed to lose some of its bitter sting. On they plodded, through flat, uneventful country until, late in the afternoon, in a sudden gleam of sunshine they came to the town of Dumfries, where Melka—although she did not know it as yet—was destined to part company with her vagabond companions.

Passing through the outskirts of the grey, stone-built town, the wanderers came to a meadow, and there, in all its glory and shining in the sudden brightness of sunshine after rain, stood Tunley's Circus!

The rain-soaked, travel-stained canvas of the 'Big Top', or main circus tent, gleamed greyly in the sun, while two rather bedraggled Union Jacks flapped bravely from the peak, with damp streamers of bright-coloured little flags strung down to the painted arch above the entrance.

All round the Big Top stood vans—their vivid blue paint and yellow wheels washed bright and clean by the rain, while 'Tunley's Circus' stood out in bold yellow lettering on the sides of each. Other long, low tents lay behind the Big Top, and it was towards these that Davy led Melka after he had unharnessed her, leaving the caravan and cart standing by the side of the road.

As they came near the tents, Melka stiffened all over and stopped dead in her tracks, with all four feet firmly planted, as the dread 'ugh-ugh-ugh' coughing roar of a lion rang out, bringing back terror-laden memories of her desert youth. She shivered all over and would have broken away, but Davy had firm hold of the halter, which he jerked impatiently.

'Come on—you!' he grunted. Then he beckoned to a small boy who was peering out of one of the vans. 'Hey, you!' he cried. 'Pedro anywhere about?'

The small boy vanished like a Jack-in-the-box, but immediately afterwards a man came out on to the wagon steps. 'Wantin' Pedro?' he asked. Then, as Davy nodded his head, he pointed slowly with the stem of his pipe to a van standing about twenty yards away. 'That's his *vardi*,' he said, and stood staring after them as Davy led Melka over to the wagon.

He hitched her to the steps and beat a tattoo on the door

with his fist. It burst open, and a slight, dark man stood framed in the doorway—a man of about twenty-eight.

'Hel-lo!' he drawled. 'So you've brought me a *prad* after all. I thought you'd forgotten.'

Without another word, he sprang lightly down the steps and stood looking at Melka. He muttered curses under his breath as he saw the places where the harness had rubbed sores on her flanks and quarters. '*Por Dios*—you gypsies!' he muttered—and then a string of strange Spanish oaths. Then he ran his hands—sure, strong, yet gentle hands—over Melka's legs, and after that, untying her from the wagon steps, he vaulted on her bare back just as he was, in trousers and a pullover jersey.

As he cantered her round the field—slow, then fast, then twisting and turning her in figures of eight—Melka recognized a master of the equestrian art: a master beside whom Dick would have appeared as a learner. As for Pedro Garcia —he was pleased enough.

Cantering back to the wagon, he slid off Melka's back, and having hitched her up to the steps again, he opened her mouth and looked at her teeth. 'A five-year-old,' he said. 'Wonder what those queer marks are!' He was looking at the tattoo marks on Melka's gums which had been stamped there when she was a foal, by a veterinary officer of the Sudan Government, to show her breeding. 'Wal!' he went on, 'come along in, and we'll talk about the *denari*!'

Ten minutes later, he and Davy came out again, and the latter slouched off looking pleased enough, while Pedro stood stroking Melka's neck, watching him go.

'Well, my little beauty!' he murmured. 'Ah, but you were cheap at the price! And now you are a circus *prad*! We will make a grand—but a *grand*—turn, you and I! In a month or two—or more—when you know your work. And now we must tidy you up! And I dare say you could do with a feed.'

Pedro Garcia, although he spoke perfect English, was a Mexican, who had spent all his youth on the pampas of the

Argentine, where he had acquired a love and mastery of horses which Melka had recognized the moment he leapt on her back. She felt it again now, in the touch of his hand as he caressed her, then loosed her halter and led her over to the stables.

The stables, a long, narrow tent, lay behind the menagerie tent, from which Melka had heard the terrifying roar of the lion, and which, in its turn, lay behind the Big Top. They passed it now, then Pedro led her through the entrance of the stables tent, and a chorus of whinnies rang out, reminding her of her welcome at Woodside Farm, and before that, of her first arrival in Khartoum.

Some dozen horses and six Shetland ponies stood in the rather greenish half-light of the tent. They stood tethered in a row on either side of the tent, their heads to the wallings, while a rope drawn between each and fastened about a foot from the ground by wooden stakes at each end, separated them from each other. A long, canvas feeding-trough, divided into partitions, ran along under their noses, while above each horse hung a net of hay.

In the middle of the tent, shining harness of every hue hung from hooks and nails driven into the tent poles, and from a rope slung from one pole to the other. White plumes and blue, and scarlet bunches of tufted feathers, also nodded from the poles, and underneath it all lay scattered the boxes, baskets and camp-beds of the tent-men—the men whose job it was to put the tents up and pull them down, prepare the arena, pack all the stuff on the wagons, and generally do the 'dirty work'.

Looming behind this forest of gay plumage, Melka suddenly caught sight of a great, grey form. It was Jumbo—the Indian elephant. He was not as big as his African brother, whom she had always feared but never caught sight of, in her youth, but as he stood twice as high as she did at the shoulder, she gazed at him with a good deal of awe, mixed with interest.

Meanwhile, Pedro called the stud groom and handed Melka over to him.

'Tie her next to Diablo,' he ordered. 'We will call her Reina—for when she is washed and groomed, she will look a queen indeed! Is it not so, my beauty?' he asked of Melka, stroking her nose as he spoke. And so Pedro Garcia recognized Melka's Royal blood.

Diablo was a black broncho—a buckjumper. He and his master had been with Tunley's Circus a little over a year, when Melka joined it. Pedro was an expert rope-spinner and lariat-thrower, and his first turn in the ring was an exhibition of skill with the lasso. Then Diablo would gallop in: Pedro would first lasso, then mount him—and then followed a thrilling exhibition of 'bronco-busting', or buckjumping.

Pedro now planned to follow up this turn with a delicate exhibition of *Haute École*, or High School riding, and it was for this that he had bought Melka. The raw, fighting, wild, black horse to be followed by a high-stepping, perfectly controlled and balanced white one! Such was his dream! But Melka had a lot to learn before that dream could come true, and the 'turn' became a fact. In the meantime, she stood in her stall next to Diablo, while a stable-boy washed and groomed her, cleaning the mud and filth of the last few weeks out of her coat, rubbing ointment into her sores, and combing her long mane and tail, while she pulled greedily at such hay as she could snatch, and listened to the black broncho's friendly chat about the other horses. In his stall he was quiet and friendly enough; it was only in the ring that he became a fighting devil!

Beyond him stood three dun resinbacks—sturdy Flemish horses, with broad, thick-set backs on which trick-riders, their feet caked with resin, performed their balancing and acrobatic feats. These three were used by a Red Indian 'turn', as was also a white resinback standing beyond. Beyond that again stood another white resinback, on whose broad back a lady rider, Fleurette, dressed in gold-spangled tights, with a diadem in her hair, performed amazing somersaults twice daily.

On the other side of the tent stood four grey Arab liberty horses and six tiny grey Shetland ponies. In the end of the tent beyond Melka stood the 'bull', Jumbo, fettered by a chain round his feet which was fastened to a stake driven well into the ground. Opposite him, six white poodles sprawled in clean straw in a big, caged-in kennel, and that, said Diablo, made up the circus troupe, when you counted the three lions and two leopards that lived in the menagerie tent next door.

When Melka first arrived, the afternoon performance was just over. So, by the time that Diablo had finished telling her all about her new companions, and the groom had made her all fresh and clean, the evening performance was almost due to start.

An air of bustle invaded the stables. First of all, stable lads got busy grooming all round, combing out manes and tails and making beautiful patterns on the quarters of the four liberty horses with a plaiting comb. Next, the Shetland ponies were harnessed into a coach, inside which, with a great deal of barking, four of the six white poodles seated themselves. Two of them were dressed in fine satin coats and breeches, the other two in brocaded skirts and bodices with bonnets tied under their chins. The remaining two, dressed as coachman and footman, mounted the box, and so they drove off past the menagerie tent, to wait for their moment to enter the ring.

When both ponies and poodles had finished their turns, and clowns were in the ring doing a 'tumbling' act, the four liberty horses were given a final polish and a last twist of the plaiting comb. Then, with scarlet head-dresses nodding above the red leather of their harness, and with a jingling of bells, they were led off, prancing, to await their turn.

There was a lull in the horse tent while a troupe of strong

men took the arena, but it was not long before the 'bull-keeper' led old Jumbo off for his act, in the second half of which the Shetland ponies again took part. Then it was Fleurette's turn on her resinback, and, after that, another display on the part of the juggling clowns made a slight pause in the bustle of the stables. No sooner had they left the ring, however, than the Redskins galloped in on their four resin-backs, and their turn was immediately followed by Pedro's lariat-throwing and lassoing display, while Diablo waited behind the curtain for the moment when he galloped on.

After that, the stables settled down for the night, although the rattle of iron buckets and the chat of the stable-boys as they watered and fed their charges and hung up the gay plumes and harness seemed a faint, last echo of the bustle that had gone on such a short time before. Through this, Melka could hear the applause which greeted a trapeze act, and then the roaring of lions and the harsh snarl of leopards, as the 'cats' padded down the iron-fenced runway which had been put up between their cages and the now caged-in arena.

By this time, Diablo and the excitable liberty horses had quietened down, and as the strains of 'God Save the King' came wafted from the Big Top, the stables were silent except for a steady, contented munching, and faint rustlings of hay and straw.

Melka lay down on her sparse bed of straw with a sigh of happiness. Even the coughing roar of a lion from the mena-gerie next door did not disturb her, and she felt nothing but thankfulness at her rescue from Davy and the rough gypsy life.

Pedro came and gave her a final pat before she slept.

She was among friends again.

(From *Melka in England*)

Many a brilliant horseman of today commenced his riding career on the humble donkey, and still retains affectionate recollections of this oft-maligned animal. The ass, largely neglected in literary spheres, has been well-served by Robert Louis Stevenson in his *Travels with a Donkey Through the Cevennes*. Modestine, infuriating, full of guile, inherently idle, is yet full of pathos. She sabotages Stevenson's travels, tries his patience to the utmost, and lacerates his sensibilities when he is forced to encourage her progress with a peasant's goad. Yet, when he parts with her, he weeps.

Modestine

(*The Horse's Poor Relation*)

BY ROBERT LOUIS STEVENSON

It remained to choose a beast of burden. Now, a horse is a fine lady among animals, flighty, timid, delicate in eating, of tender health; he is too valuable and too restive to be left alone, so that you are chained to your brute as to a fellow galley-slave; a dangerous road puts him out of his wits; in short, he's an uncertain and exacting ally, and adds thirty-fold to the troubles of the voyager. What I required was something cheap and small and hardy, and of a stolid and peaceful temper, and all these requisites pointed to a donkey.

There dwelt an old man in Monastier, of rather unsound intellect according to some, much followed by street boys, and known to fame as Father Adam. Father Adam had a cart, and to draw the cart a diminutive she-ass, not much bigger than a dog, the colour of a mouse, with a kindly eye and a determined underjaw. There was something neat and high-bred, a quakerish elegance, about the rogue that hit my fancy on the spot. Our first interview was in Monastier market-place. To prove her good temper, one child after another was set upon her back to ride, and one after another went head over heels into the air; until a want of confidence began to reign in youthful bosoms, and the experiment was discontinued from a dearth of subjects. I was already backed by a deputation of my friends, but, as if this were not enough, all the buyers and sellers came round and helped me in the bargain, and the ass and I and Father Adam were the centre of a hubbub for near half an hour. At length she passed into my service for the consideration of sixty-five francs and a glass of brandy. The sack had already cost eighty francs and two glasses of beer, so that Modestine, as I instantly baptized her, was upon all accounts the cheaper article. Indeed, that was as it should be, for she was only an appurtenance of my mattress, or self-acting bedstead on four castors.

I had a last interview with Father Adam in a billiard-room at the witching hour of dawn, when I administered the brandy. He professed himself greatly touched by the separation, and declared he had often bought white bread for the donkey when he had been content with black bread for himself, but this, according to the best authorities, must have

my effects. The

and I was to w

bread, and an o

mutton, and the

elaborate system

fatuous content.

above the donkey

on a brand-new

fit the animal,

might be expecte

a very careless tr

That elaborate sy

many sympathise

they tightened th

time would have

be hauling with

that one thought i

can make a more

enthusiastic groom

misadventure of t

and I went forth f

slaughter.

The bell of Mon

of these preliminar

the common. As I c

secret shame and t

me from tampering

her four small hoo

time to time she s

so small under the

got across the ford

about the matter,

other bank, where

woods, I took in m

with a quaking sp

brisked up her pac

lapsed into her former minuet. Another application had the same effect, and so with the third. I am worthy the name of an Englishman, and it goes against my conscience to lay my hand rudely on a female. I desisted, and looked her all over from head to foot; the poor brute's knees were trembling and her breathing was distressed; it was plain that she could go no faster on a hill. God forbid, thought I, that I should brutalize this innocent creature; let her go at her own pace, and let me patiently follow.

What that pace was, there is no word mean enough to describe; it was something as much slower than a walk as a walk is slower than a run; it kept me hanging on each foot for an incredible length of time; in five minutes it exhausted the spirit and set up a fever in all the muscles of the leg. And yet I had to keep close at hand and measure my advance exactly upon hers, for if I dropped a few yards to the rear, or went on a few yards ahead, Modestine came instantly to a halt and began to browse. The thought that this was to last from here to Alais nearly broke my heart. Of all conceivable journeys, this promised to be the most tedious. I tried to tell myself it was a lovely day; I tried to charm my foreboding spirit with tobacco, but I had a vision ever present to me of the long, long roads, up hill and down dale, and a pair of figures ever infinitesimally moving, foot by foot, a yard to the minute, and, like things enchanted in a nightmare, approaching no nearer to the goal.

In the meantime there came up behind us a tall peasant, perhaps forty years of age, of an ironical snuffy countenance, and arrayed in the green tail-coat of the country. He overtook us hand over hand, and stopped to consider our pitiful advance.

'Your donkey,' says he, 'is very old?'

I told him, I believed not.

Then, he supposed, we had come far.

I told him, we had but newly left Monastier.

'*Et vous marchez comme ça!*' cried he, and, throwing back his head, he laughed long and heartily. I watched him, half

prepared to feel offended, until he had satisfied his mirth;
and then, 'You must have no pity on these animals' said
he, and, plucking a switch out of a thicket, he began to lace
Modestine about the sternworks, uttering a cry. The rogue
pricked up her ears and broke into a good round pace, which
she kept up without flagging, and without exhibiting the
least symptom of distress, as long as the peasant kept beside
us. Her former panting and shaking had been, I regret to
say, a piece of comedy.

My *deus ex machinâ*, before he left me, supplied some excellent, if inhumane, advice, presented me with the switch,
which he declared she would feel more tenderly than my
cane, and finally taught me the true cry or masonic word
of donkey-drovers, 'Proot!' All the time, he regarded me
with a comical, incredulous air, which was embarrassing
to confront, and smiled over my donkey-driving, as I might
have smiled over his orthography, or his green tail-coat. But
it was not my turn for the moment.

I was proud of my new lore, and thought I had learned the
art to perfection. And certainly Modestine did wonders for
the rest of the forenoon, and I had a breathing space to look
about me. It was Sabbath; the mountain-fields were all
vacant in the sunshine, and as we came down through St
Martin de Frugères, the church was crowded to the door,
there were people kneeling without upon the steps, and the
sound of the priest's chanting came forth from the dim
interior. It gave me a home feeling on the spot, for I am a
countryman of the Sabbath, so to speak, and all Sabbath
observances, like a Scottish accent, strike in me mixed feelings, grateful and the reverse. It is only a traveller, hurrying
by like a person from another planet, who can rightly enjoy
the peace and beauty of the great ascetic feast. The sight of
the resting country does his spirit good. There is something
better than music in the wide unusual silence, and it disposes
him to amiable thoughts, like the sound of a little river or
the warmth of sunlight.

I hurried over my midday meal, and was early forth again. But, alas, as we climbed the interminable hill upon the other side, 'Proot!' seemed to have lost its virtue. I prooted like a lion, I prooted mellifluously like a sucking-dove; but Modestine would be neither softened nor intimidated. She held doggedly to her pace; nothing but a blow would move her, and that only for a second. I must follow at her heels, incessantly belabouring. A moment's pause in this ignoble toil, and she relapsed into her own private gait. I think I never heard of anyone in as mean a situation. I must reach the lake of Bouchet, where I meant to camp, before sundown, and, to have even a hope of this, I must instantly maltreat this uncomplaining animal. The sound of my own blows sickened me. Once, when I looked at her, she had a faint resemblance to a lady of my acquaintance who formerly loaded me with kindness; and this increased my horror of my cruelty.

To make matters worse, we encountered another donkey, ranging at will upon the roadside; and this other donkey chanced to be a gentleman. He and Modestine met nickering for joy, and I had to separate the pair and beat down their young romance with a renewed and feverish bastinado. If the other donkey had had the heart of a male under his hide, he would have fallen upon me tooth and hoof, and this was a kind of consolation—he was plainly unworthy of Modestine's affection. But the incident saddened me, as did everything that spoke of my donkey's sex.

It was blazing hot up the valley, windless, with vehement sun upon my shoulders, and I had to labour so consistently with my stick that the sweat ran into my eyes. Every five minutes, too, the pack, the basket and the pilot-coat would take an ugly slew to one side or the other, and I had to stop Modestine, just when I had got her to a tolerable pace of about two miles an hour, to tug, push, shoulder, and re-adjust the load. And at last, in the village of Ussel, saddle and all, the whole hypothec, turned round and grovelled in the dust below the donkey's belly. She, none better pleased, incontinently drew up and seemed to smile, and a party of one man, two women and two children came up, and, standing round me in a half-circle, encouraged her by their example.

I had the devil's own trouble to get the thing righted, and the instant I had done so, without hesitation, it toppled and fell down upon the other side. Judge if I was hot! And yet not a hand was offered to assist me. The man, indeed, told me I ought to have a package of a different shape. I suggested, if he knew nothing better to the point of my predicament, he might hold his tongue. And the good-natured dog agreed with me smilingly. It was the most despicable fix. I must plainly content myself with the pack for Modestine, and take the following items for my own share of the portage: a cane, a quart flask, a pilot-jacket heavily weighted in the pockets, two pounds of black bread, and an open basket full of meats and bottles. I believe I may say I am not devoid of greatness of soul, for I did not recoil from this infamous burden. I disposed it, Heaven knows how, so as to be mildly portable, and then proceeded to steer Modestine through the village. She tried, as was indeed her invariable habit, to enter every house and every courtyard in the whole length, and, encumbered as I was, without a hand to help myself, no words can render an idea of my difficulties. A priest, with six or seven others, was examining a church in process of repair, and he and his acolytes laughed loudly as they saw my plight. I had seen good men struggling with adversity in the person of a jackass, and the recollection filled me with penitence. That was in my old light days, before this trouble came upon me. God knows at least that I shall never laugh again, thought I. But oh, what a cruel thing is a farce to those engaged in it!

A little out of the village, Modestine, filled with the demon, set her heart upon a by-road, and positively refused to leave it. I dropped all my bundles, and, I am ashamed to say,

struck the poor sinner twice across the face. It was pitiful
to see her lift up her head with shut eyes, as if waiting for
another blow. I came very near crying, but I did a wiser
thing than that, and sat down squarely by the roadside to
consider my situation under the cheerful influence of tobacco
and a nip of brandy. Modestine, in the meanwhile, munched
some black bread with a contrite, hypocritical air. It was
plain that I must make a sacrifice to the gods of shipwreck.
I threw away the empty bottle destined to carry milk; I
threw away my own white bread, and, disdaining to act by
general average, kept the black bread for Modestine; lastly,
I threw away the cold leg of mutton and the egg-whisk,
although this last was dear to my heart. Thus I found room
for everything in the basket, and even stowed the boating-
coat on the top. By means of an end of cord I slung it under
one arm, and although the cord cut my shoulder, and the
jacket hung almost to the ground, it was with a heart greatly
lightened that I set forth again.

I had now an arm free to thrash Modestine, and cruelly I
chastised her. If I were to reach the lakeside before dark she
must bestir her little shanks to some tune. Already the sun
had gone down into a windy-looking mist, and although
there were still a few streaks of gold far off to the east on the
hills and the black firwoods, all was cold and grey about our
onward path. . . . I promise you, the stick was not idle. I
think every decent step that Modestine took must have cost
me at least two emphatic blows. There was not another
sound in the neighbourhood but that of my unwearying
bastinado.

Suddenly, in the midst of my toils, the load once more bit
the dust, and, as by enchantment, all the cords were simul-
taneously loosened, and the road scattered with my dear
possessions. The packing was to begin anew from the beginning, and as I had to invent a new and better system, I do
not doubt but I lost half an hour. . . . My shoulder was cut, so
that it hurt sharply; my arm ached like toothache from

perpetual beating; I gave up the lake and my design to camp. . . .

Blessed be the man who invented goads! Blessed the innkeeper of Bouchet St Nicolas, who introduced me to their use! This plain wand, with an eighth of an inch of pin, was indeed a sceptre when he put it in my hands. Thenceforward Modestine was my slave. A prick, and she passed the most inviting stable door. A prick, and she broke forth into a gallant little trotlet that devoured the miles. It was not a remarkable speed, when all was said, and we took four hours to cover ten miles at the best of it. But what a heavenly change since yesterday! No more wielding of the ugly cudgel; no more flailing with an aching arm; no more broadsword exercise, but a discreet and gentlemanly fence. And what although now and then a drop of blood should appear on Modestine's mouse-coloured wedge-like rump? I should have preferred it otherwise, indeed, but yesterday's exploits had purged my heart of all humanity. The perverse little devil, since she would not be taken with kindness, must even go with pricking. . . .

The next innkeeper had begun life as a muleteer, and when I came to charge Modestine (the next morning) showed himself full of the prudence of his art. 'You will have to change this package,' said he; 'it ought to be in two parts and then you might have double the weight.'

I explained that I wanted no more weight, and that for no donkey hitherto created would I cut my sleeping-bag in two.

'It fatigues her, however,' said the innkeeper; 'it fatigues her greatly on the march. Look.'

Alas, there were her two forelegs no better than raw beef on the inside, and blood was running from under her tail. They told me when I started, and I was ready to believe it, that before a few days I should come to love Modestine like a dog. Three days had passed, we had shared some misadventures, and my heart was still as cold as a potato towards my beast of burden. She was pretty enough to look at, but then she had given proof of dead stupidity, redeemed indeed by patience, but aggravated by flashes of sorry and ill-judged light-heartedness. And I own this new discovery seemed another point against her. What the devil was the good of a she-ass if she could not carry a sleeping-bag and a few necessaries? I saw the end of the fable rapidly approaching, when I should have to carry Modestine. Aesop was the man to know the world! I assure you I set out with heavy thoughts upon my short day's march. . . .

I had hurried to the topmost powers of Modestine, for I dearly desired to see the view upon the other side before the day had faded. But it was night when I reached the summit; the moon was riding high and clear, and only a few grey streaks of twilight lingered in the west. Modestine and I— it was our last meal together—had a snack upon the top of St Pierre—I on a heap of stones, she standing by me in the moonlight and decorously eating bread out of my hand. The poor brute would eat more heartily in this manner, for she had a sort of affection for me, which I was soon to betray.

On examination, next morning, Modestine was pronounced unfit for travel. She would need at least two days' repose, according to the ostler; but I now was eager to reach Alais for my letters, and, being in a civilized country of stage-coaches, I determined to sell my lady-friend and be off by the diligence that afternoon. Our yesterday's march, with the testimony of a driver who had pursued us up the long hill of St Pierre, spread a favourable notion of my donkey's capabilities. Intending purchasers were aware of an unrivalled opportunity. Before ten I had an offer of twenty-five francs, and before noon, after a desperate engagement, I sold her, saddle and all, for five-and-thirty. The pecuniary gain is not obvious, but I had bought freedom into the bargain.

It was not until I was fairly seated by the driver, and rattling through a rocky valley with dwarf olives, that I became aware of my bereavement. I had lost Modestine.

Up to that moment I had thought I hated her; but now she was gone,

> *'And, oh,*
> *The difference to me!'*

For twelve days we had been fast companions; we had travelled upwards of a hundred and twenty miles, crossed several respectable ridges, and jogged along with our six legs by many a rocky and many a boggy by-road. After the first day, though sometimes I was hurt and distant in manner, I still kept my patience, and as for her, poor soul! she had come to regard me as a god. She loved to eat out of my hand. She was patient, elegant in form, the colour of an ideal mouse, and inimitably small. Her faults were those of her race and sex; her virtues were her own. Farewell, and if for ever——

Father Adam wept when he sold her to me; after I had sold her in my turn, I was tempted to follow his example, and being alone with a stage-driver and four or five agreeable young men, I did not hesitate to yield to my emotion.

(From *Travels with a Donkey*)

A Grown-up Could Hardly have Stood It

WHAT interested me in our new neighbourhood was not the
school, nor the room I was to have in the house all to myself
but the stable which was built back of the house. My father
let me direct the making of a stall, a little smaller than the
other stalls, for my pony, and I prayed and hoped and my
sister Lou believed that that meant that I would get the
pony, perhaps for Christmas. I pointed out to her that there
were three other stalls and no horses at all. This I said in
order that she should answer it. She could not. My father,
sounded, said that some day we might have horses and a
cow; meanwhile a stable added to the value of a house.
'Some day' is a pain to a boy who lives in and knows only
'now'. My good little sisters, to comfort me, remarked that
Christmas was always coming and grown-ups were always

talking about it, asking you what you wanted and then giving you what they wanted you to have. Though everybody knew what I wanted, I told them all again. My mother knew that I told God, too, every night: I wanted a pony, and to make sure that they understood, I declared that I wanted nothing else.

'Nothing but a pony?' my father asked.

'Nothing,' I said.

'Not even a pair of high boots?'

That was hard. I did want boots, but I stuck to the pony. 'No, not even boots.'

'Nor candy? There ought to be something to fill your stocking with, and Santa Claus can't put a pony into a stocking.'

That was true, and he couldn't lead a pony down the chimney either. But no. 'All I want is a pony,' I said. 'If I can't have a pony, give me nothing, nothing.'

Now I had been looking myself for the pony I wanted, going to sales stables, inquiring of horsemen, and I had seen several that would do. My father let me 'try' them. I tried so many ponies that I was learning fast to sit on a horse. I chose several, but my father always found some fault with them. I was in despair. When Christmas was at hand I had given up all hope of a pony, and on Christmas Eve I hung up my stocking along with my sisters', of whom, by the way, I now had three. I haven't mentioned them or their coming because, you understand, they were girls, and girls, young girls, counted for nothing in my manly life. They did not mind me either; they were so happy that Christmas Eve that I caught some of their merriment. I speculated on what I'd get; I hung up the biggest stocking I had, and we all went reluctantly to bed to wait till morning. Not to sleep; not right away. We were told that we must not only sleep promptly, we must not wake up till seven-thirty the next morning—or if we did, we must not go to the fireplace for our Christmas presents. Impossible.

We did sleep that night, but we woke up at six a.m. We lay in our beds and debated whether to obey till, say, half-past six. Then we bolted. I don't know who started it, but there was a rush. We all disobeyed; we raced to disobey and get first to the fireplace in the front room downstairs. And there they were, the gifts, all sorts of wonderful things, mixed-up piles of presents; only, as I disentangled the mess, I saw that my stocking was empty; it hung limp; not a thing in it; and under and around it—nothing. My sisters had knelt down, each by her pile of gifts; they were squealing with delight, till they looked up and saw me standing there in my night-gown with nothing. They left their piles to come to me and look with me at my empty place. Nothing. They felt my stocking; nothing.

I don't remember whether I cried at that moment, but my sisters did. They ran with me back to my bed, and there we all cried till I became indignant. That helped some. I got up, dressed, and driving my sisters away, I went alone out into the yard, down to the stable, and there, all by myself, I wept. My mother came out to me by and by; she found me in my pony stall, sobbing on the floor, and she tried to comfort me. But I heard my father outside; he had come part way with her, and she was having some sort of angry quarrel with him. She tried to comfort me; besought me to come to breakfast. I could not; I wanted no comfort and no break-fast. She left me and went on into the house with sharp words for my father.

I don't know what kind of a breakfast the family had. My sisters said it was 'awful'. They were ashamed to enjoy their own toys. They came to me, and I was rude. I ran away from them. I went around to the front of the house, sat down on the steps, and, the crying over, I ached. I was wronged, I was hurt—I can feel now what I felt then, and I am sure that if one could see the wounds upon our hearts, there would be found still upon mine a scar from that terrible Christmas morning. And my father, the practical joker, he must have been hurt too, a little. I saw him looking out of the window. He was watching me or something for an hour or two, drawing back the curtain ever so little lest I catch him, but I saw his face, and I think I can see now the anxiety upon it, the worried impatience.

After—I don't know how long—surely an hour or two—I was brought to the climax of my agony by the sight of a man riding a pony down the street, a pony and a brand-new saddle, the most beautiful saddle I ever saw, and it was a boy's saddle; the man's feet were not in the stirrups, his legs were too long. The outfit was perfect; it was the realization of all my dreams, the answer to all my prayers. A fine new bridle, with a light curb bit. And the pony! As he drew near, I saw that the pony was really a small horse, what we called an Indian pony, a bay, with black mane and tail, and one white foot and a white star on his forehead. For such a horse as that I would have given, I could have forgiven, anything.

But the man, a dishevelled fellow with a blackened eye and a fresh-cut face, came along, reading the numbers on the houses, and, as my hopes—my impossible hopes—rose, he looked at our door and passed by, he and the pony, and the saddle and the bridle. Too much. I fell upon the steps, and having wept before, I broke now into such a flood of tears that I was a floating wreck when I heard a voice.

'Say, kid,' it said, 'do you know a boy called Lennie Steffens?'

I looked up. It was the man on the pony, back again at our horse block.

'Yes,' I spluttered through my tears. 'That's me.'

'Well,' he said, 'then this is your horse. I've been looking all over for you and your house. Why don't you put your number where it can be seen?'

'Get down,' I said, running out to him.

He went on saying something about 'ought to have got here at seven o'clock; told me to bring the nag here and tie him up to your post and leave him for you. But I got into a drunk—and a fight—and a hospital, and——'

'Get down,' I said.

He got down, and he boosted me up to the saddle. He offered to fit the stirrups for me, but I didn't want him to. I wanted to ride.

'What's the matter with you?' he said angrily. 'What you crying for? Don't you like the horse? He's a dandy, this horse. I know him of old. He's fine at cattle; he'll drive 'em home.'

I hardly heard, I could scarcely wait, but he persisted. He adjusted the stirrups, and then, finally, off I rode, slowly, at a walk, so happy, so thrilled, that I did not know what I was doing. I did not look back at the house or the man, I rode off up the street, taking note of everything—of the reins, of the pony's long mane, of the carved leather saddle. I had never seen anything so beautiful. And mine! I was going to ride up past Miss Kay's house. But I noticed on the horn of the saddle some stains like raindrops, so I turned and trotted home, not to the house but to the stable. There was the family, father, mother, sisters, all working for me, all happy. They had been putting in place the tools of my new business: blankets, curry-comb, brush, pitchfork—everything, and there was hay in the loft.

'What did you come back so soon for?' somebody asked. 'Why didn't you go on riding?'

I pointed to the stains. 'I wasn't going to get my new saddle rained on,' I said. And my father laughed. 'It isn't raining,' he said. 'Those are not raindrops.'

'They are tears,' my mother gasped, and she gave my father a look which sent him off to the house. Worse still, my mother offered to wipe away the tears still running out of my eyes. I gave her such a look as she had given him, and she went off after my father, drying her own tears. My sisters remained and we all unsaddled the pony, put on his halter, led him to his stall, tied and fed him. It began really to rain, so all the rest of that memorable day we curried and combed that pony. The girls plaited his mane, forelock and tail, while I pitchforked hay to him and curried and brushed, curried and brushed. For a change we brought him out to drink; we led him up and down, blanketed like a race-horse; we took turns at that. But the best, the most inexhaustible fun, was to clean him. When we went reluctantly to our midday Christmas dinner we all smelt of horse, and my sisters had to wash their faces and hands. I was asked to, but I wouldn't, until my mother bade me look in the mirror. Then I washed up—quick. My face was caked with the muddy lines of tears that had coursed over my cheeks to my mouth. Having washed away that shame, I ate my dinner, and as I ate I grew hungrier and hungrier. It was my first meal that day, and as I filled up on the turkey and stuffing, the cranberries and the pies, the fruit and the nuts—as I swelled, I could laugh. My mother said I still choked and sobbed now and then, but I laughed, too; I saw and enjoyed my sisters' presents till—I had to go out and attend to my pony, who was there, really and truly there, the promise, the beginning, of a happy double life. And—I went and looked to make sure —there was the saddle, too, and the bridle.

But that Christmas, which my father had planned so carefully, was it the best or the worst I ever knew? He often asked me that; I could never answer as a boy. I think now that it was both. It covered the whole distance from broken-hearted misery to bursting happiness—too fast. A grown-up could hardly have stood it.

(From *The Autobiography of Lincoln Steffens*)

The Highwayman's Mare

BY R. D. BLACKMORE

'YOUR mare,' said I, standing stoutly up, being a tall boy now; 'I never saw such a beauty, sir. Will you let me have a ride of her?'

'Think thou could'st ride her, lad? She will have no burden but mine. Thou could'st never ride her. Tut! I would be loth to kill thee.'

'Ride her!' I cried with the bravest scorn, for she looked so kind and gentle; 'there never was horse upon Exmoor foaled but I could tackle in half an hour. Only I never ride upon saddle. Take them leathers off her.'

He looked at me with a dry little whistle, and thrust his hands into his breeches pockets, and so grinned that I could not stand it. And Annie laid hold of me in such a way that I was almost mad with her. And he laughed and approved her for doing so. And the worst of all was—he said nothing.

'Get away, Annie, will you? Do you think I am a fool, good sir? Only trust me with her and I will not override her.'

'For that I will go bail, my son. She is liker to override thee. But the ground is soft to fall upon, after all this rain. Now come out into the yard, young man, for the sake of your mother's cabbages. And the mellow straw bed will be softer for thee, since pride must have its fall. I am thy mother's cousin, boy, and am going up to house. Tom Faggus is my name, as everybody knows, and this is my young mare, Winnie.'

What a fool I must have been not to know it at once! Tom Faggus, the great highwayman, and his young blood mare, the strawberry! Already her fame was noised abroad, nearly as much as her master's, and my longing to ride her grew tenfold, but fear came at the back of it. Not that I had the smallest fear of what the mare could do to me, by fair play and horse-trickery, but that the glory of sitting upon her seemed to be too great for me, especially as there were rumours abroad that she was not a mare after all, but a witch. However, she looked like a filly all over, and wonderfully beautiful, with her supple stride, and soft slope of shoulder, and glossy coat beaded with water, and prominent eyes, full of love or of fire. Whether this came from her Eastern blood of the Arabs newly imported, and whether the cream colour, mixed with our bay, led to that bright strawberry tint, is certainly more than I can decide, being chiefly acquainted with farm horses. And these come of any colour and form; you can never count what they will be, and are lucky to get four legs to them.

Mr Faggus gave his mare a wink, and she walked demurely after him, a bright young thing, flowing over with life, yet dropping her soul to a higher one, and led by love to anything, as is the manner of females, when they know what is best for them. Then Winnie trod lightly upon the straw, because it had soft muck under it, and her delicate feet came back again.

'Up for it still, boy, be ye?' Tom Faggus stopped and the mare stopped there, and they looked at me provokingly.

'Is she able to leap, sir? There is good take-off on this side of the brook.'

Mr Faggus laughed very quietly, turning round to Winnie, that she might enter into it. And she, for her part, seemed to know exactly where the joke was.

'Good tumble-off, you mean, my boy. Well, there can be small harm to thee. I am akin to thy family, and know the substance of their skulls.'

'Let me get up,' said I, waxing wroth, for reasons I cannot tell you because they are too manifold; 'take off your saddle-bag things. I will try not to squeeze her ribs in, unless she plays nonsense with me.'

Then Mr Faggus was up on his mettle, at this proud speech of mine; and John Fry was running up all the while, and Bill Dadds, and half a dozen. Tom Faggus gave one glance around, and then dropped all regard for me. The high repute of his mare was at stake, and what was my life compared to it? Through my defiance, and stupid ways, here was I in a dullo, and my legs not come to their strength yet, and my arms as limp as a herring.

Something of this occurred to him, even in his wrath with me, for he spoke very softly to the filly, who now could scarce subdue herself; but she drew in her nostrils, and breathed to his breath, and did all she could to answer him.

'Not too hard, my dear,' he said; 'let him gently down on the mixen. That will be quite enough.'

Then he turned the saddle off, and I was up in a moment. She began at first so easily, and minced about as if pleased to find so light a weight on her, that I thought she knew I could ride a little, and feared to show any capers. 'Gee wugg, Polly,' cried I, for all the men were now looking on, being then at the leaving-off time. 'Gee wugg, Polly, and show what thou be'est made of.' With that I plugged my heels into her, and Billy Dadds flung his hat up.

Nevertheless, she outraged not, though her eyes were frightening Annie, and John Fry took a pick to keep him safe; but she curbed to and fro, with her strong fore-arms rising, like springs ingathered, waiting and quivering grievously, and beginning to sweat about it. Then her master gave a shrill, clear whistle, when her ears were bent towards him, and I felt her form beneath me gathering up like whalebone, and her hind legs coming under her, and I knew that I was in for it.

First she reared upright in the air, and struck me full on the nose with her comb, till I bled worse than Robin Snell made me, and then down with her forefeet deep in the straw, and her hind-feet going for heaven. Finding me sticking to her still like wax (for my mettle was up as hers was), away she flew with me, swifter than ever I went before, or since, I trow. She drove full-head at the cob wall—'Oh, Jack, slip off,' screamed Annie—then she turned like light, when I thought to crush her, and ground my left knee against it. 'Mux me,' I cried, for my breeches were broken, and short words went the farthest—'If you kill me, you shall die with me.' Then she took the courtyard gate at a leap, knocking my words between my teeth, and then right over a quickset hedge, as if the sky were a breath to her; and away for the water meadows, while I lay on her neck like a child at the breast and wished I had never been born. Straight away, all in the front of the wind, and scattering clouds around her, all I knew of the speed we made was the frightful flash of her shoulders, and her mane like trees in a tempest. I felt the earth under us rushing away, and the air left far behind us, and my breath came and went, and I prayed to God and was sorry to be so late of it.

All the long, swift while, without power of thought, I clung to her crest and shoulders, and dug my nails into her creases, and my toes into her flank-part, and was proud of holding on so long though sure of being beaten. Then in her fury at feeling me still, she rushed at another device for it and leaped the wide water-trough sideways across, to and fro, till no breath was left in me. The hazel bough stook me too hard in the face, and the tall dog-briars got hold of me, and the ache of my back was like crimping a fish; till I longed to give up, and lay thoroughly beaten, and lie still there and die in the creases. But there came a shrill whistle from up the home-hill, where the people had hurried to watch us; and the mare stopped as if with a bullet; then set off for home with the speed of a swallow, and going as smoothly and silently. I never had dreamed of such delicate motion, fluent, and graceful, and ambient, soft as the breeze flitting over the flowers, but swift as the summer lightning. I sat up again, but my strength was all spent, and no time left to recover it, and at last, as she rose at our gate like a bird, I tumbled off into the mixen.

(From *Lorna Doone*)

Three Hunting Songs

THE CLIPPER THAT STANDS IN THE STALL AT THE TOP

Go strip him, lad! Now, sir, I think you'll declare
Such a picture you never set eyes on before;
   He was bought in at Tatt's for three hundred I swear,
And he's worth all the money to look at, and more;
     For the pick of the basket, the show of the shop,
     Is the Clipper that stands in the stall at the top.

In the records of racing I read their career,
There were none of the sort but could gallop and stay;
   At Newmarket his sire was the best of his year,
And the Yorkshiremen boast of his dam to this day;
     But never a likelier foal did she drop
     Than this Clipper that stands in the stall at the top.

A head like a snake, and a skin like a mouse,
An eye like a woman, bright, gentle and brown,
   With loins and a back that would carry a house,
And quarters to lift him smack over a town!
     What's a leap to the rest, is to him but a hop,
     This Clipper that stands in the stall at the top.

When the country is deepest, I give you my word
'Tis a pride and a pleasure to put him along;
  O'er fallow and pasture he sweeps like a bird,
And there's nothing too wide, nor too high, nor too strong;
  For the ploughs cannot choke, nor the fences can crop,
  This Clipper that stands in the stall at the top.

Last Monday we ran for an hour in the Vale,
Nor a bullfinch was trimmed, of a gap not a sign!
  All the ditches were double, each fence had a rail,
And the farmers had locked every gate in the line;
  So I gave him the office, and over them—Pop!
  Went the Clipper that stands in the stall at the top.

I'd alead of them all when we came to the brook,
A big one—a bumper—and up to your chin;
  As he threw it behind him, I turned for a look,
There were eight of us had it, and seven got in!
  Then he shook his lean head when he heard them go plop!
  This Clipper that stands in the stall at the top.

E'er we got to the finish, I counted but few,
And never a coat without dirt, but my own;
  To the good horse I rode all the credit was due,
When the others were tiring, he scarcely was blown;
  For the best of the pace is unable to stop
  The Clipper that stands in the stall at the top.

You may put on his clothes; every sportsman, they say,
In his lifetime has one that outrivals the rest,
  So the pearl of *my* casket I've shown you today,
The gentlest, the gamest, the boldest, the best;
  And I never will part, by a sale or a swop,
  With my Clipper that stands in the stall at the top!

THE GOOD GREY MARE

Oh! once I believed in a woman's kiss,
   I had faith in a flattering tongue;
For lip to lip was a promise of bliss,
   When lips were smooth and young.
But now the beard is grey on my cheek,
   And the top of my head gets bare,
So little I speak, like an Arab Sheikh,
   But put my trust in my mare.

For loving looks grow hard and cold,
   Fair hands are turned away,
When the fruit has been gathered—the tale been told,
   And the dog has had his day;
But chance and change 'tis folly to rue,
   And say I, the devil may care!
Nor grey nor blue are so bonny and true
   As the bright brown eye of my mare!

It is good for a heart that is chilled and sad
   With the death of a vain desire,
To borrow a glow that shall make it glad
   From the warmth of a kindred fire.
And I leap to the saddle, a man indeed;
   For all I can do and dare,
In the power and speed that are mine at need,
   While I sit on the back of my mare!

With the fair wide heaven above outspread
   The fair wide plain to meet,
With the lark and his carol high over my head,
   And the bustling pack at my feet—
I feel no fetter, I know no bounds,
   I am free as a bird in the air;
While the covert resounds, in a chorus of hounds,
   Right under the nose of the mare.

We are in for a gallop—away! away!
    I told them my beauty could fly;
And we'll lead them a dance e'er they catch us today,
    For we *mean* it, my lass and I!
She skims the fences, she scours the plain,
    Like a creature winged, I swear,
With snort and strain, on the yielding rein;
    For I'm bound to humour the mare.

They have pleached it strong, they have dug it wide,
    They have turned the baulk with the plough;
A horse that can cover the whole in its stride
    Is cheap at a thousand, I vow;
So I draw her together, and over we sail,
    With a yard and a half to spare—
Bank, bullfinch and rail—'tis the curse of the vale,
    But I leave it all to the mare!

Away! away! they've been running to kill,
    With never a check from the find;
Away! away! we are close to them still,
    And the field are *furlongs* behind!
They can hardly deny they were out of the game,
    Lost half 'the fun of the fair',
Though the envious blame and the jealous exclaim,
    'How that old fool buckets his mare!'

Who—whoop! they have him—they're round him; how
    They worry and tear when he's down!
'Twas a stout hill-fox when they found him, now
    'Tis a hundred tatters of brown!
And the riders arriving as best they can,
    In panting plight, declare,
That 'First in the van was the old grey man,
    Who stands by his old grey mare.'

I have lived my life—I am nearly done—
    I have played the game all round;
But I freely admit that the best of my fun
    I owe it to horse and hound.
With a hopeful heart and a conscience clear,
    I can laugh in your face, Black Care;
Though you're hovering near, there's no room for you here,
    On the back of my good grey mare.

THE PLACE WHERE THE OLD HORSE DIED

In the hollow by the pollard where the crop is tall and rank
    Of the dock-leaf and the nettle growing free,
Where the bramble and the brushwood straggle blindly
    o'er the bank,
    And the pyat jerks and chatters on the tree,
    There's a fence I never pass
    In the sedges and the grass
But for very shame I turn my head aside,
    While the tears come thick and hot,
    And my curse is on the spot—
'Tis the place where the old horse died.

There's his hoof upon the chimney, there's his hide upon
    the chair,
    A better never bent him to the rein;
Now, for all my love and care, I've an empty stall and bare;
    I shall never ride my gallant horse again!
      How he laid him out at speed,
      How he loved to have a lead,
How he snorted in his mettle and his pride!
      Not a flyer of the Hunt
      Was beside him in the front,
At the place where the old horse died!

Was he blown? I hardly think it. Did he slip? I cannot tell.
    We had run for forty minutes in the vale,
He was reaching at his bridle; he was going strong and well,
    And he never seemed to falter or to fail;
        Though I sometimes fancy, too,
        That his daring spirit knew
The task beyond the compass of his stride,
        Yet he faced it true and brave,
        And dropped into his grave
At the place where the old horse died.

I was up in half a minute, but he never seemed to stir,
    Though I scored him with my rowels in the fall;
In his life he had not felt before the insult of the spur,
    And I knew that it was over, once for all.
        When motionless he lay
        In his cheerless bed of clay,
Huddled up without an effort on his side—
        'Twas a hard and bitter stroke
        For his honest back was broke,
At the place where the old horse died.

With a neigh so faint and feeble that it touched me like a
    groan,
    'Farewell,' he seemed to murmur, 'e'er I die':
Then set his teeth and stretched his limbs, and so I stood
    alone,
    While the merry chase went heedless sweeping by.
        Am I womanly and weak
        If the tear was on my cheek
For a brotherhood that death could thus divide?
        If sickened and amazed
        Through a woeful mist I gazed
On the place where the old horse died?

There are men both good and wise who hold that in a future
    state
  Dumb creatures we have cherished here below
Shall give us joyous greeting when we pass the golden gate;
    Is it folly that I hope it may be so?
      For never man had friend
      More enduring to the end,
Truer mate in every turn of time and tide.
      Could I think we'd meet again
      It would lighten half my pain
At the place where the old horse died.
            (From *G. J. Whyte-Melville's Hunting Songs*.)

Mr Jorrocks Crosses a Country

BY R. S. SURTEES

'TALLY HO!' now screamed Jorrocks, as a magnificent fellow in a spotless suit of ruddy fur now crossed the ride before him at a quiet, stealing, listening sort of pace, and gave a whisk of his well-tagged brush on entering the copse-wood across.

'Hoop! hoop! hoop! hoop!' roared Mr Jorrocks, putting his finger in his ear, and holloa-ing as loud as ever he could shout; and just as he got his horn fumbled past his guard, Dexterous, Affable and Mercury dashed across the ride, lashing their sterns and bristling for blood, and Pigg appeared a little below, cantering along with the rest of the pack at his horse's heels.

'Here, Pigg! There, Pigg!' roared Mr Jorrocks. 'Just by the old hoak-stump. *Gently*, now! ah, ware'eel—that's not the vay of him; he's hover to the left, I tells ye. That's him! Mercury has him. Hoick to Mercury, hoick *get away, get away, get away*, 'ounds! Hoick together! hoick together! Oh, Pigg, what a whopper he is!' observed Mr Jorrocks, as Pigg joined him in the ride. 'The biggest fox whatever was seen —if we do but kill him—my vig! I'll eat his tongue for supper. Have it grilled "*cum grano salis*", with a *lee*-tle Cayenne pepper, as Pomponius Hego would say.'

'Aye,' replied Pigg, grinning with delight, his cap-peak in the air and the tobacco juice streaming down his mouth like a Chinese mandarin. '*Ar'll be the death of a shillin*' mysel'!' Saying which he hustled his horse and turned to his hounds.

Away they go again, full cry across the covert to the utmost limits, and then back again to the far side. Now the fox takes a full swing round, but won't quit—now he cuts across—now Mr Jorrocks views him and swears he'll have his brains as well as his tongue for supper. Pigg has him next, and again comes Mr Jorrocks's turn. 'Dash my vig, but he's a tough 'un!' observed Mr Jorrocks, to James Pigg, as they met again on the rising ground at the top of the rise, where Mr Jorrocks had been fifteen times, and Pigg seventeen, both their horses streaming with perspiration, and the blue and yellow worsted fronts of their bridles embossed with foam. 'Dash my vig, but it's a million and a half of petties,' continued Mr Jorrocks, looking at his watch and seeing it wanted twenty minutes to four, 'that we adwertised, for there's a wast o' go in him yet, and he'll take the shine out of some of our hounds before he's done with them —send them dragglin' 'ome with their sterns down—make 'em cry *capevi*', I'm thinkin'.'

'Niver fear!' exclaimed Pigg. 'Niver fear!—whativer ye do keep Tamboureen a rowlin'—yonder he gans! ar wish it mayn't be a fresh 'un. Arn't draggled a bit . . .'

A sudden pause ensues—all still as death—not a note— not even a whimper!

'*Who-oop!*' exclaims Mr Jorrocks in ecstasies. '*Who-oop!* I say—heard the leadin' 'ound crack his back. Old Cruiser for a guinea!'

'*Yonder they gan!*' cried Pigg, pointing to a hog-backed hill on the left, over which three couples of hounds were straining to gain the body of the pack—saying which he clapped spurs to his horse and set off at full gallop, followed by Charles.

'Oh dear! Oh, dear!' exclaimed Mr Jorrocks, the picture of despair. 'Wot shall I do? Wot shall I do? Gone away at this hour—strange country—nobody to pull the 'edges down for me or catch my 'oss if I gets spilt, and there's that Pigg riding as though there was not never no such man as his master. Pretty kettle of fish!' continued Mr Jorrocks, trotting on the line they had taken. A bridle gate let him out of cover, and from the first hill our master sees his hounds going like pigeons over the large grazing grounds of Beddington Bottoms, with Pigg and Stobbs a little in the rear, riding as hard as ever their horses can lay legs to the ground.

''Ow that Scotch beggar rides!' exclaimed Mr Jorrocks, eyeing Pigg going straight as an arrow, which exclamation brought him to his first fence at the bottom of the hill, over which both horsemen had passed without disturbing a twig.

''OLD UP, 'oss!' roared Mr Jorrocks, seizing the reins and whip with one hand and the cantel of the saddle with the other, as Arterxerxes floundered through a low fence with a little runner on the far side. 'OLD UP!' repeated he, as they got scrambled through, looking back and saying, 'Terrible nasty place—wonders I ever got over! Should ha' been drund to a certainty if I'd got in. Wouldn't ride at it again for nothin' under a knighthood—Sir John Jorrocks, Knight!' continued he, shortening his hold of his horse. 'And my ladyship Jorrocks!' added he. 'She'd be bad to 'old —shouldn't wonder if she'd be for goin' to Halmack's! Dash my buttons, but I wish I was off this beastly fallow,' continued he; 'wonderful thing to me that the farmers can't see there'd be less trouble i' growin' grass than in makin' these nasty rutty fields. 'Eavens be praised, there's a gate— and a lane too,' saying which he was speedily in the latter, and gathering his horse together he set off at a brisk trot in the direction he last saw the hounds going.

Terribly deep it was, and great Arterxerxes made a noise like the drawing of corks as he blobbed along through the stiff, holding clay.

Thus Mr Jorrocks proceeded for a mile or two more, until

he came upon a red-cloaked gypsy wench stealing sticks from a rotten fence on the left.

''Ave you seen my 'ounds, ould gal?' inquired he, pulling up short.

'Bless your beautiful countenance, my cock angel!' exclaimed the woman in astonishment at the sight of a man in a scarlet coat with a face to match. 'Bless your beautiful countenance, you're the very babe I've been looking for all this blessed day—cross my palm with a bit o' siller, and I'll tell you *sich* a fortin!'

'CUSS YOUR FORTIN!' roared Mr Jorrocks, sticking his spurs into his horse, and grinning with rage at the idea of having pulled up to listen to such nonsense.

'I hope you'll brick your neck, you nasty, ugly ould thief!' rejoined the gypsy, altering her tone.

''Opes I *sharn't*,' muttered Mr Jorrocks, trotting on to get out of hearing. Away he went, blob, blob, blobbing through the deep holding clay as before.

Presently he pulled up again with a 'Pray my good man, 'ave you seen my 'ounds—Mr Jorrocks's 'ounds, in fact?' of a labourer scouring a fence gutter. 'Don't you 'ear me, man?' bellowed he, as the countryman stood staring with his hand on his spade.

'I be dull of hearing, sir,' at length drawled the man, advancing very slowly towards our master with his hand up.

'Oh dear! Oh dear!' exclaimed Mr Jorrocks, starting off again. 'Was there ever sich a misfortinate indiwidual as John Jorrocks? 'Ark! Vot's that? Pigg's 'orn! Oh, dear, only a cow! Come hup, 'oss, I say, you hugly beast!—there surely was never such a worthless beast lapped in leather as you,' giving Arterxerxes a good double-thonging as he spoke.

'Pray, my good man,' then inquired he of a drab-coated, big-basketed farmer on a bay cart-horse, whom he suddenly encountered at the turn of the road, ''ave you seen anything of my 'ounds?—Mr Jorrocks's 'ounds, in fact?'

'Yes, sir,' replied the farmer, all alive; 'they were running past Langford plantations with the fox dead beat close afore them.'

''Ow long since, my friend?' inquired Mr Jorrocks, brightening up.

'Oh, just as long as it's taken me to come here—mebbe ten minutes or a quarter of an hour, not longer certainly. If you put on you may be in at the death yet.'

(From *Handley Cross*)